Unbridled Fate

A Trilogy

When Fate Rumbles (Book One)

By Stephen J. Flitcraft

Unbridled Fate
A Trilogy
When Fate Rumbles (Book One)
By Stephen J. Flitcraft
© 2013 Brass Hinge Publishing

ISBN: 978-0-9831590-7-0 (Printed version)

ISBN: 978-0-9831590-8-7 (E-book version)

The poem "Mothers" © 2011 Stephen J. Flitcraft

Note: This is a work of fiction. Names, characters, businesses, places, events, and incidents are a product of the author's imagination. Any resemblance to actual persons, living or dead, or actual events is purely coincidental. Some of the cities and towns named are real; however, their descriptions, locations, and or representations may not be, necessarily, accurate.

Acknowledgements

Brass Hinge Publishing Marion, IN
"Putting Words in Your Mind!"

Website: brasshingepublishing.com

Book cover design: BHP Productions

Consulting: Debra Ratliff

Front cover photo: "Girl behind glass" is from shutterstock.com

Back cover photos: "Girl on bench" & "Ominous sky" are from shutterstock.com

See other fine books by Stephen J. Flitcraft at the end of this book

Visit: brasshingepublishing.com

Chapter One
Twister of Fate

Sarah drove to one of her favorite childhood places, the city park. She had always loved the playground, especially on the days when her mom accompanied her.

She sat on an out-of-the-way bench and basked in the warm afternoon sun. Consumed with delight, she thought, *"It seems like it was only yesterday that Mom and I was here."*

Childhood memories danced in her head. She took in a refreshing breath of air and held it. *"We had so much fun."* She shook her head with regret, released her breath, and wiped away a happy tear.

She heard giggling and squealing in the distance. She turned and could see several children playing on the merry-go-round. She leaned back, closed her eyes, put her face toward the warm sun, and listened to the sounds of the park.

Just as she was thinking that it was such a peaceful day, her heart broke. She remembered, *"Today is the anniversary of Mom's death."*

Saddened by the memory, she put her arm on the back of the bench, laid her head against her shoulder, and scanned the park.

She whispered, "The trees that survived the tornados have mended their wounds . . .

And they are still standing . . .

The grass is still green . . .

The children still play . . .

And the sky is still blue."

She shut her eyes again, but nothing could soothe the emptiness she felt. She whimpered, "Yes, Mom; I know, and life still goes on.

I miss you so much."

Suddenly, something nudged her hand. She screamed mildly, quickly looked, and jerked her arm away. The gentle bump came from the cold wet nose of a dog. Her heart raced. A young man, who was standing close by, was holding the dog's leash. She looked at the man with a friendly, yet uncertain smile. She reached out for the dog, hoping to pet it before it moved away. The man was watching her, and gave a silent nod of approval.

Sarah gently stroked the dog's back and then gave it a loving hug. She looked up again when the young man gave an apology. "I'm sorry. I hope she didn't scare you."

Sarah smiled reassuringly, and patted the dog on the head. "That's okay." The dog wagged its tail and licked her hand. She ruffled the dog's ears, looked at the man again, and praised, "Your dog is beautiful!"

The young man simply nodded, tugged the leash, and commanded, "Come on, Lacy, let's go!"

The man and his dog walked on, and it was quiet again.

Sarah smiled at a squirrel that was sitting on the grass watching her. She spoke softly. "I've enjoyed your company, Little Fella."

The squirrel kept a close eye on Sarah and nibbled on an acorn. Then, without reason, her little friend bristled its tail, dropped the empty shell, and scampered away.

Sarah frowned when she heard sirens in the distance. The screeching, almost haunting, noises broke the tranquility.

Anxiety crept in as she remembered the terrible day, when suddenly, her life crashed head-on with reality. Memories of the howling winds and rolling thunder flashed through her head. Deep fear taunted her. She closed her eyes and put her trembling hands over her face. She tried to block the raging storm from her mind, but the attempt was futile.

She wept, and tears flowed down her face. She shook her head in anguish.

[One year earlier]

Tina was amazed at the destruction as she drove slowly through the Westfield neighborhood. She was in awe of the amount of damage caused by the storm. Soft music flowed from the radio.

As the music faded out, a deep voiced commentator spoke. "This is a Saturday news update, from the Jet, WJET Radio in Westfield, Ohio.

Finally folks, there is some welcome news for many Westfield residents. Officials from the Ohio Power and Electric Company have released new information concerning power restoration."

Tina turned up the volume and continued to listen.

"As of 7:25 this morning, crews from Ohio Power and Electric have restored electricity to nearly 1500 residents of Westfield. This leaves only 400 homes without power.

Federal officials from the National Weather Service have determined that, seven days ago, two F4 tornados raged across Clark and Joseph counties. The late-night storms flattened homes and buildings in a mile-wide swath of destruction through neighborhoods on the West and North sides of Westfield. The total number of deaths caused by those tornados is now 37.

In other news..."

Tina turned down the radio as she pulled in to the driveway of her dearest friend Sarah. She noticed that the huge maple tree which once stood in the front yard is now gone. The cement sidewalk is heaving from where the massive root ball emerged from the ground when the giant relic fell. Tina saw small piles of sawdust. Not a single twig remained from where the fallen tree had laid.

Sarah was sitting on her roofless front porch. She stood up when Tina's truck stopped.

Sarah walked to Tina and hugged her tightly. Sarah sniffled, and tears flowed from her eyes.

Tina gave Sarah a long hug. "I am so sorry about your mom. Is there anything I can do to help?"

Sarah released her hug. "No. I'll be fine. The hardest part was the funeral. Thank you for being there for me."

Tina assured, "That's what friends are for. I'll always be here for you."

Sarah took a deep breath, and then quickly released it. "Boy, Mom always said the same thing." Sarah raised her hand in disbelief and exclaimed, "Look now at what's happened; Mom's gone!"

Tina apologized, "I'm sorry. I didn't mean to upset you."

Sarah shook her head slightly. "You didn't upset me. It's just that . . ." She waved her hand, shook her head again, and replied, "Oh, never mind!

It's so good to see you!"

Tina pointed at the truck. "My brother loaned me his pick-up for a few days. I stopped by to let you know that I will be here first thing in the morning to help you with your mom's house. Maybe we can get it all in one trip."

Sarah smiled grimly. "Mom had a lot of things. I haven't been over there to sort through any of them."

Tina hugged Sarah again. "It's okay. We'll get it, even if it takes all day. Besides, it'll be a Sunday. If you still need me, I can help on Monday as well"

Sarah smiled. "You are such a good friend, and a real trooper."

Tina replied, "Hey, we'll take it one bit at a time, and before you know it, we'll be done. I have plenty of boxes to bring, and I found a few old canvas tarps we can use."

Tina arrived early on Sunday. She noticed Sarah was a little perkier and not so stressed out.

Tina dreads the type of work they will do, but being a lifelong friend of Sarah's, she could never let her down, especially now.

Sarah sat on the truck seat. "Are you ready for a long day?"

Tina smiled and proclaimed, "I am, if you are."

Sarah nodded. "Yes, I suppose I am, but only because I'm expected to be." She looked at Tina, frowned slightly, and confided, "I know I must do this, but I'm so not looking forward to it."

Tina said, "There's no time like the present. So, My Friend, let's be going." Sarah nodded in agreement.

Tina drove them to the north side neighborhood where Sarah's mother had lived. She backed in the driveway at an angle. She eased the truck across the lawn, stopping short of the front entry. Tina stepped out of the truck, paused, and looked up. She pointed. "It amazes me how the house next door looks as though nothing happened, and your mom's house is so torn up." She cranked her neck and looked up even farther. She exclaimed, "Oh my, her roof is gone, too!"

Sarah rested her arms on the hood of the truck. She looked up and shook her head. "I'd say everything upstairs is gone. The only things left that might be worth saving will be whatever we find downstairs."

Tina turned toward Sarah and leaned against the truck. She asked, "What are you going to do with the house? Are you going to rebuild it, or maybe move in to it yourself?"

Sarah answered quickly, "Oh my, I could never live in this house, knowing Mom died here. I may see if the house is fixable and sell it, or, I may have it torn down and sell the lot. I'm not sure."

Tina grabbed a handful of boxes from the back of the truck. "We'd better get busy, or we'll never get done." She walked toward the house.

Sarah smiled, picked up the remaining boxes and tarps, and followed. "Okay, I'm ready. Let's do it!"

Inside, they discovered that the immense rains of the storm had ruined all the furniture. Even after a week, the carpet still held water. The wet rug squished beneath their shoes as they walked across it.

Sarah stopped and began to cry. She muttered, "The rain has ruined everything; there's nothing left!"

Tina consoled, "I'm sure we can find some things of value that survived. I'd guess there are many things you might want to keep. Let's put a tarp on the floor, and one over this couch. That should keep our boxes from getting soaked."

Tina headed for the kitchen. "I'll go in here and see what I can find."

Sarah went to her mother's first floor bedroom. She slowly opened the closet door. Wet insulation littered the clothing. The drywall ceiling had fallen in. Debris filled the shoes on the floor. She looked up. There was a small stack of photos sitting on a shelf. They were all in frames. She took them down and set them on the dresser. The top picture was from many years ago. It was of her and her mother on Easter Sunday. She whispered, "I was only eight years old." She touched the glass. "I was so thrilled to get a new dress. Mom was so beautiful."

She reached up on the shelf and took down a stack of books. The books were totally soaked. Disheartened, she tossed them in the middle of the floor, and murmured, "I'll throw them away later." She stood on her tiptoes and looked for anything else that might be on the shelf. She saw a metal box sitting in the back corner. She could barely touch it. She jumped up and snatched it off the shelf. There were no markings or labels on it. She tried to open it. "Damn; it'slocked!"

She thought, "There must be a key here somewhere." She pulled a chair over to the closet and climbed up. She saw a key taped to the back wall. She peeled the tape away and retrieved the key. She sat down on the chair, and put the key in the slot. The instant she turned the key, the lid sprung open. The unexpected flip of the lid startled her, and she nearly dropped the box.

Inside the box was a diamond ring, a set of pearl earrings, and two large envelopes. Scotch tape held the envelopes shut. The once clear tape had yellowed with age. The letters, addressed to James and Jennifer Meeks, had return addresses for the judicial offices of the State of Ohio.

Sarah opened the first envelope and pulled out the papers. Intensely curious, she quietly read the letter.

"From the Office of Child Welfare

Dear James and Jennifer Meeks,

We have sent this letter to inform you that the Division of Child Welfare is requesting for you to appear in regard to final custody and the adoption of Sarah Lynn, a nine-week-old baby girl."

Sarah, stunned by what she read, whispered, "Custody; adoption; oh; My God!"

She read on. "This letter is not a summons; however, I believe it would be in your best interest to appear before the court. In a few days, I will send legal documentation and directives from the Adoption Division for the State of Ohio. You must answer any further questions the judge may have about your case. Barring unforeseen circumstances, I believe that on the day of your appearance, final custody of Sarah Lynn will be yours.

I am aware that this has been a long and tedious process. I applaud your patience and unwavering desire to adopt a child. I congratulate your successful participation in the Adoption Program of the State of Ohio.

Sincerely,

Secretary for the Judicial Offices of the State of Ohio,
Amanda K. Rutledge"

Dazed by the news, Sarah put the letter up to her face and repeated, "Oh my God, I'm an adopted child!"

She sat motionless, trying to comprehend what the letter meant.

Tina came in to the bedroom. She saw Sarah sitting very still and staring at the wall. "Sarah, are you okay?"

Sarah slowly turned. She handed the letter to Tina. "Read this!"

Tina took the letter and silently read it.

She exclaimed, "Adoption! What the hell is this?"

Sarah touched the open box. "That letter was in here." She pointed at the closet. "The box was on the upper shelf. It was locked, but I found the key taped to the back wall." She held up the other letter. "When I opened the box, it had these letters in it."

Tina's jaw dropped. "Jim and Jen are not your real dad and mom?"

There was a long quiet pause as they stared at each other. In silent desperation, they tried to grasp the situation.

Sarah took a deep breath and let it out. "I'm so confused. I don't know what to say, or even think!

My God, Mom is gone, and Dad is gone. I have so many questions, but now, I may never know the answers!" She gave a helpless look towards Tina. She shook her head slowly. "I'm not sure that I even want to know the answers." She put her hands over her face, and then opened them. She gave Tina a doubtful look and argued with herself. "But I must try to find out . . . Shouldn't I?

But where would I start?" She looked in Tina's eyes, hoping for a clue.

Tina held the letter in one hand and pointed at the signature with the other. "I'd say you need to find this Amanda Rutledge. She apparently works at the state office building in Columbus. To me, she'd be the first person I'd want to talk to."

Sarah nodded, thought for a moment, and then admitted, "Because of Mom's death, I've taken an extended leave of absence from my job. I suppose I could go to Columbus on Monday or Tuesday."

Tina nodded. "Tuesday would be great; that's one of my days off. I'd be able to go with you, that is, if you would like for me to tag along."

Sarah smiled. "I always enjoy your company. You know that."

Tina gave another quick nod. "Okay then, we'll go to Columbus on Tuesday."

Sarah added, "We'll make a day of it. Maybe we can find a nice restaurant. It'll be my treat."

Tina smiled in agreement. "You have a deal. I'll pick you up Tuesday at 8:00 in the morning."

Tina clasped her hands together. "For now, we need to get all this stuff packed and taken to the storage building." She pointed with her thumb toward the kitchen. "I'm almost done in there, but I need your help with one of the big boxes." She opened her eyes wide and laughed softly. "It amazes me how much a couple stacks of cast-iron skillets can actually weigh."

Tina left the room.

Sarah put the letter back in the envelope and placed it in the box with the other things. She closed the lid, and held the box against her chest. She looked up, shook her head slightly, and asked, "Mom, why didn't you tell me about this?"

Sarah continued to gather mementos, silently deciding the value and eventual fate of each item. Her mind churned. Unanswered questions troubled her. It was difficult to concentrate. The emotional turmoil made the already unpleasant task even harder.

She heard Tina shout from the kitchen. "Hey, we're in luck! I found a battery-operated radio. Maybe we can have a little music to entertain us?"

Sarah heard the static noises of the radio as Tina searched for a clear station. Music suddenly began, and Tina hollered, "Oh good, we can listen to my favorite station. Is that okay with you?"

Sarah looked toward the kitchen, smiled slightly, but said nothing.

She walked to the living room, sat on a chair, and began to cry.

Tina heard Sarah weeping and went to her. She cradled Sarah and kissed her cheek. "My God, you must be at your wit's end. I'm so sorry."

Tears flowed down Sarah's cheeks. She whimpered, "I'm sorry, but I can't do this anymore, at least not today. I'm so confused. I can't even think straight. Can we load up whatever is ready, and go?

Please?"

Tina said with encouragement, "We sure can. You sit right here, and I'll load up these boxes."

Tina went to the kitchen.

Suddenly, she popped her head back in the living room. "Umm, somebody packed half a house in this one box! I'm going to need some help with it."

Despite her despair, Sarah chuckled, wiped away her tears, and went to help.

They loaded the truck with everything that was ready. Tina tried to shut the back window of the topper, but the glass would have to rest against a box that didn't quite fit all the way in. She looked at Sarah and shrugged her shoulders. "Hmm." She asked, "Do you think it'll be okay to ride this way?"

Sarah nodded yes, and said, "Let's go."

Tina started the truck and put it in gear. She was ready to drive away, but a police car pulled in and blocked her path. Tina looked at Sarah and put the truck in park.

An officer got out of the cruiser. He grabbed a sack from the front seat, and approached Sarah's side of the truck.

Sarah recognized the officer and said, "It's Kelly McGregor. We call him Chancy. He's been a friend of my mom and dad for years."

Sarah opened her door, jumped out of the truck, and threw her arms around Kelly. "It's good to see you, Chancy."

Chancy spoke in a very distinct Irish accent. "You're looking good, Little Lassie. I'm so sad to hear about your mother; it's such an unexpected tragedy."

Sarah reassured, "Yes, but I'll be okay."

He said, "God bless you, Child.

I will miss your mother so very much. She'll be in my prayers." He pointed at Sarah. "And you too. God said it was time for Ms. Jenny to go with him, and so it will be.

You know, Miss Sarah, your mother was very proud of you."

Sarah showed a grim smile. "Yes, she told me those same words many times." She hugged Chancy again. "Thank you so much for your thoughts and prayers."

Chancy held the sack out for her to see. "I have a gift for you." He opened the bag and pulled out a plaque. He handed it to her, and explained, "I know how much you loved your mother. I am so sad that Ms. Jenny is gone. I always had a soft spot in my heart for her. It may not seem like much, but I wrote a poem in her honor. I had it engraved on this plaque." He handed it to Sarah. "I want you to have it."

Sarah smiled and accepted the gift. "This is wonderful. I didn't know you were a poet?"

Chancy waggled his head and said, "Well, I'm not a real poet." He pointed at the engraving on the plaque. "These words popped in my head, so I wrote them down. I was so pleased with the result; I had this keepsake made for you."

Sarah held the plaque to her breast and hugged Chancy again. "Awwww; thank you so much, you are such a sweetheart."

Chancy kissed the tip of his forefinger and touched Sarah's lips with it. "I have to run, Little Lady. If you need me for anything, please call." He backed away. "You be careful!"

Sarah blew Chancy a kiss.

Sarah and Tina chimed together, "Good bye!"

Sarah sat in the truck again and closed the door.

Tina said, "He is so sweet." She leaned toward Sarah to get a better look at the plaque. "What does it say?"

Sarah smiled. "At the very top, in large letters, it says, "Mothers." She continued reading the poem:

Mothers

A mother's time is never done.

Even though her day has come.
Spreading love for all these years,

Now it's time we shed a tear.

A tear of joy as love abounds,

She now strolls on angels ground.

God has known her heart's intent.

She'll spread the love where others went.
Heaven's gate is pearl and white;

Streets of gold and angel light.

Serene and calm and zephyrs blow.

Eternal glory she will know.

God has whisked her from our earth.

Now angels see how mothers were.

Moms are angels, of God's disguise.

Pillars of strength, so sure and wise.

Revealed to angels who awe and aspire,

Reveled and honored in a place much higher.

With these words, I'm sure you agree,

Mothers will be angels in heaven, indeed.

By Kelly McGregor

Tina said in awe, "That's a beautiful poem. Chancy did very well."

Sarah closed her eyes and smiled. "Yes, he did.

Bless his heart."

As Tina drove on, Sarah rested the plaque on her lap.

In the next block, Chancy was leaning on his car. He was keeping an eye on the neighborhood.

Tina honked as she passed by. Sarah waved.

Tina suggested, "How about if I stop someplace where we can enjoy a nice afternoon cocktail? It'll be a well-deserved reward for two hard-working cleaner uppers. The drinks are on me."

Sarah nodded. "Yes, I could definitely use a little something to slow my brain down."

Sarah shook her head and thought, *"Boy, what a day this has been. What else could happen? Surely, I'm not the only one in the universe whose world is crumbling around them."*

Tina reached over and turned up the volume of the radio.

Sarah's thoughts melted into the flood of music.

Chapter Two
Bump in the Night

Tina drove to the storage building where she and Sarah unloaded the truck. When finished, Tina noticed, "Boy, there is plenty of room left in this unit."

They got in the truck to leave. Sarah set the metal box on the seat between them.

Tina slumped back in her seat and exclaimed, "What a day!"

Sarah agreed, "Yes, what a day it has been. I could definitely use a nice rum and coke to help cut the edge off this stressful day."

Tina agreed, "Yes, maybe a, couple-three, stiff drinks will do the trick for me too?"

Tina drove to the Paramount Pub. She parked the truck near the front entrance. She grabbed her purse and headed inside. Sarah picked up her purse and the metal box, and followed.

The Paramount Pub is a popular nighttime place to gather. The out-of-the-way bar is small, cozy, and clean. Tina and Sarah prefer the Paramount to many others because fun spoiling troublemakers rarely visit the quiet bar. The food here is great and reasonably priced. It has no pool table or game machines. The only entertainment comes from a dimly lit vintage-style jukebox.

They sat at their favorite table.

Sheila, the gray-haired bar owner, recognized them. She quipped, "Gee girls, isn't it a little early in the day to be out hunting a date?"

Tina grinned. "We're not out on the hunt, as you put it. We came here because this bar is so homey feeling. All we want is a little peace and quiet. Your bar was a little out of the way, but we decided the atmosphere would be well worth the extra time it would take to get here."

Sheila smiled. "Well, thank you for coming."

Tina gave thumbs up, and said, "No problem."

Sheila gave Sarah a sad look. "I'm so sorry to hear about your mother. It's such a terrible thing to have happen." She began shaking her head in dismay, but then switched to a nod of encouragement. "If you need anything, you be sure to let me know. I'll be glad to help you in any way I can."

Sarah replied gratefully, "Thank you, Sheila. You are so kind. And yes, it was quite a shock, but I'll be okay."

Sarah put her hands on her cheeks. "Let me see, umm, may I have a very tall, and very potent, rum and coke."

Sheila nodded.

Tina cringed slightly, but agreed, "Yes, I'll have the same, but please, make mine not as strong." She put her hand on her chest and admitted, "I'm driving."

Sheila brought the drinks and set them on the table. "These are on me. Do you want me to turn up the jukebox?"

Sarah said, "Maybe a little, but please, not too loud."

Sarah set the metal box on the table. She sipped her drink and stared at the box.

She set her drink aside, and reached to open the box.

Tina put a firm hand on top of it. "You don't have to do this. You've been through enough for one day."

Sarah dragged the box from beneath Tina's hand. "I know, but I want to see what the other letter has to say." She opened the box and removed both letters. She chose the one she hadn't read, unfolded it, and quickly scanned it.

When finished, she handed the letter to Tina. "This is the original paperwork which started the adoption process. I noticed, too, it's signed by Amanda Rutledge, the same as the other letter."

Sarah removed the pearl earrings from the box. She held them up and said, "Mom hardly ever wore jewelry. She would wear these for special occasions like Christmas, Easter, or her anniversary. I always wondered where she kept them." She took the ring from the box and slid it on the end of her index finger. She showed it to Tina. "This is her engagement ring. It was very special to her. She always said she would never get rid of it." Sarah clutched the ring in her palm and said, "Her wedding set went to the grave with her."

Tina sympathized, "Awe, you don't have to explain things to me. I understand."

Sarah replied, "I don't mind talking about it, especially with a friend."

Tina changed the subject. "I will pick you up on Tuesday morning, and we'll go to the Judicial Building in Columbus. If we can find Amanda Rutledge, maybe she'll be able to tell us more about your past."

Sarah reached up and scratched her head. "I have so many questions." She held her hand palm up. "My problem is I'm not sure where to begin."

Tina put her elbow on the table and her hand on her chin. "I'm thinking that the first good question would be, why?" She sipped her drink and watched Sarah.

Sarah stated further, "Yes, why, and who, and where are my real parents?"

Tina ordered another round of drinks.

They sat and talked for hours about the many possibilities.

Who might Sarah's parents actually be?

Could her real parents still be alive?

Where was she born?

There were so many questions and very few avenues to find the answers.

The evening crowd began filtering in to the pub. Two friends joined Tina and Sarah. Time flew, and the drinks flowed. Soon, it was time to head home.

Tina drove. She stopped in front of Sarah's house, but did not shut off the engine. She looked at Sarah and moaned, "I am so tired. It's been a long night."

Sarah worried. "Please, be careful driving home."

Tina hugged Sarah, and assured, "Don't worry, I'll be okay."

Sarah reached out and squeezed Tina's shoulder. She looked her in the eyes and demanded softly, "You'd better be, I don't need another disaster in my life."

Sarah stepped out of the truck and shut the door. Tina waved good-bye, and drove away. Sarah watched until the glow of the tail lights had faded in to the night. She turned and trudged toward the house.

She was exhausted, and went directly to her bed. She flopped down and put her face in the pillow. She rolled over, pulled a blanket across her chest, and fell asleep.

After what seemed only a few minutes, Sarah opened her eyes. The bedroom seemed different in some way, yet, it was so peaceful. She noticed that she was floating above her bed. She saw herself, lying there. She had experienced this before, so she didn't panic.

Cautiously, she tried to move around the room. Her body drifted toward the wall. She tried to stop, but bumped into the wall and caromed to the left. She giggled at her misjudged motion. She gathered her thoughts and drifted back to a spot above the bed. There, like a ballerina, she twirled in midair. She smiled because she knew that in a few minutes, she would be with her mom again.

She covered her eyes, and with excited anticipation, began thinking of a special day. It was a wonderful Christmas morning of long ago, when two of her childhood dreams had come true.

She felt the air rush across her face as she whisked away to a faraway time.

In what seemed like an instant, she heard her mom say, "Sarah, please come and open your gift."

Sarah saw herself, as a little girl, run across the room and in to the arms of her mom.

Sarah remembered the gift. It was a doll, which could walk across the floor by itself. Sarah watched, and could feel the joy all over again.

Her mother said, "Now, Little Girl, you have a baby to take care of . . . the same as me." Her mother hugged little Sarah.

Sarah watched them, and could feel the warmth of her mother's arms. A tear rolled down Sarah's cheek. She missed her mother so much.

Sarah watched again as her mother, with little Sarah in arms, spun in a circle.

Her mom said, "Soon, Sweetheart, you will be in ballet school."

Little Sarah screamed with delight. She hugged and kissed her mom.

Sarah could remember the softness of her mother's face. She thought, *"Yes, soft as angel's wings."*

Sarah was happy that once again she had fulfilled her whim. Nonetheless, it was time to return to her body.

As soon as that thought entered her mind, she rose up in the bed. She put her hands over her face and smiled between them. "Number 14 . . . Oh My God, another one!" She plopped back on her pillow, closed her eyes, and whispered a wish. "I hope they never stop." Her heart pounded heavily. She opened her eyes and spoke reverently. "Mom, I can hardly wait for another time when I will be with you." She pulled the warm blanket over her body, closed her eyes, and tried to calm her excitement.

She eventually fell back to sleep.

Sarah awoke in the early morning hours. She had to force herself to get out of bed. She plodded to the kitchen, poured a cup of coffee, and sat in a chair at the table. Her first cup of the day seemed more of a necessity than it did the usual morning pleasure. She glimpsed at the clock. "9:00 already? Gee, where did the night go?"

She heard a knock on the front door. The knob turned and the door opened. Tina spoke out, "Sarah, I'm here, are you awake?"

Sarah hollered, "I'm in here. Come get a fresh cup of coffee."

Tina came to the kitchen, got a cup from the upper cabinet, and poured herself some coffee. She leaned back against the counter and looked at Sarah. She asked, "Are you feeling okay? My word, you look so tired."

Sarah said, "I had another foolish dream last night."

Tina took a sip of her coffee and listened.

Sarah explained further. "It was so weird. I dreamed that I was floating above my bed. I could see myself lying there. I wouldn't call it a nightmare, but, afterward, I could hardly sleep."

Tina confided, "Wow, I have those too! My friend calls them Out of Body Experiences. During the past year or so, I've had several of them."

Sarah leaned up in her chair. "You've had this type of dream, too? I've had 14 of them, and that's only the ones I can remember since I began counting." She sipped her coffee. "They are calm and peaceful to me." She held up her index finger. "I also found out that during these dreams, I can control where I am. What I mean is, if I'm above the bed and want to move over by the window, all I have to do is think about it, and my body flies over there. It's kind of cool." She asked, "Do you know what causes them?"

Tina shivered. "I don't like them. They scare me. My friend says they are not dreams; they're events that happen when your spirit leaves your body. It sounded creepy to me, so I didn't ask much more about it." She raised her eyebrows and said, "They scared me so bad that I'd wake up immediately." She sipped the last of her coffee and turned away to refilled her cup.

Sarah held her cup out, and Tina topped it off.

Tina set the coffee pot back in the coffee machine. "My friend gave me the name of a man who is writing a book about Out of Body Experiences. I remember the author's name as being Dr. Sheffield, but I'm not certain. If you want his information, I'll find it for you. Maybe this Dr. Sheffield can help."

Sarah agreed, "Yes, I'd like to get the address and phone number. I definitely want to know more about these out-of-body experiences, or dreams, or nightmares, or whatever they are." Tina said, "You got it. I'll call you tonight."

Sarah went to get dressed.

Tina and Sarah headed out to finish their chore from the previous day. Tina drove.

Sarah turned down the volume of the radio. "Are we still going to the capitol?"

Tina replied, "Tomorrow is Tuesday, right?" She confirmed, "You can bet we are." She quipped,

"Besides, I'm curious to find out more about you . . . now that we're not sure who you really are!"

Sarah gave Tina a friendly swat and said, "Stop it! You know who I am!"

Sarah pinched her lower lip and thought, "*Yes, I'm very curious, too!*" She leaned back in her seat and stared out the window.

Tina turned up the volume of the radio, and then reached over and squeezed Sarah's hand. "I am sure we will find out some interesting things."

Sarah thought, "*I hope we can find Amanda Rutledge.*"

Chapter Three
Finding Amanda

Tina and Sarah arrived in Columbus sooner than they had planned. In a way, arriving early was a blessing; there was no pressure to find a parking place.

Sarah pointed at a parking garage that was next to the capitol building. She noticed, "Look, next to the parking garage is Jan's Café."

Tina suggested, "We might as well park there. We can walk to Jan's for a cup of coffee. Are you hungry?"

Sarah admitted, "I'm too nervous to eat, but, if you're hungry, I won't mind if you grab a bite."

Tina nodded. "Maybe some toast will hold me over until later. If Jan's has good food, we'll do lunch there, too."

Tina found a spot to park on the third floor of the garage. They walked down to the Café.

They found an empty table, and soon, a friendly waitress came by. She set two cups on the table and filled them with hot coffee. The girl smiled and introduced herself. "Good morning. My name is Wendy. I'll be your server today." She held up the pot of coffee. "You're in luck. This is a fresh pot. Do either of you need cream or sugar?"

Suddenly, Sarah remembered, "Damn, I left those letters in the car." She stood up and said to

Tina, "Give me your keys; I'll go get them." She looked at Wendy and said, "No cream or sugar for me." She smiled at Tina and said, "I'll be right back."

Tina denied the cream and sugar, too.

Wendy smiled at Tina. "I'll take your order when your friend gets back."

Wendy turned and walked away.

A huffing and puffing Sarah returned with the letters. She sat down, gasping for air. "Whew, managing three flights of stairs is a real bear."

Tina snickered, "Aww, you poor baby! Are you not in shape anymore?"

Sarah crinkled her nose and replied, "Duh?" She caught her breath and sipped her coffee.

Wendy returned and took their orders. Tina opted for a donut instead of toast. Sarah decided not to eat.

Tina asked Wendy, "Do you know what time we can enter the capitol building?"

Wendy looked at her watch. "It's only 8:15. The capitol building won't be open to the public until 9:00. By the way, they will check your purses for cell phones, or, for that matter, anything that might pose a danger."

Tina said, "Crap, I should have known there would be strict security, especially in a state building."

Sarah nodded. "Boy, we're brain-dead today!"

Tina added, "I guess we'll have to take our phones back to the car before we go in the building."

Sarah growled, "Damn it, I'll have to make another trip up all those stairs!" She pointed a stern finger at Tina and whimpered childishly, "You should have parked on the ground floor!"

Wendy turned to walk away, nodded her head, and giggled. She mumbled, "Yep, you should have!"

Tina and Sarah made the trek back up the stairs to leave there phones in the car. They returned to the café, had another cup of coffee, and then headed to the Capitol building. By then, it was well after 9:00.

After clearing security, they found the elevators, which were down the hall. Tina paused to read the list of floors and rooms that was on a plaque beside the elevators. She pointed. "There it is, Judicial Offices, fourth floor, room 460." They rode the elevator to the fourth floor. A young female receptionist was tending the information desk. She greeted them with a friendly smile. "Hello."

Sarah asked, "Can you help us? We need to find a Mrs. Amanda Rutledge."

The girl scanned a sheet of paper. She shook her head. "I'm sorry; I find no Amanda Rutledge listed."

Sarah said, "I believe she works for the State Adoption Division, or possibly a similar department."

The girl commented, "We have a Division of Child Welfare; I believe they handle adoption issues."

Sarah agreed, "Yes, we can start there, I suppose."

The girl pointed down a corridor and directed, "Room 489 is down the first hall to your right. It is nearly at the end. It will be just past the bathrooms on the left."

Tina and Sarah found the room. This time, an elderly gray-haired woman, who appeared past the age of 60, was talking on a phone. The woman looked up when they stopped at her desk. The woman smiled, held up a finger, and silently mouthed the words, "One moment."

Sarah nodded slightly. She and Tina backed away a few feet.

The woman hung up the phone and asked, "How may I help you?"

Sarah took the letters from her purse and handed them to the woman. "I am looking for Amanda Rutledge. Can you help me?"

The woman scanned the letters and handed them back to Sarah. "I'm sorry, but Amanda is now retired.

Those letters are from the Judicial Offices, and the Division of Child Welfare. They concern adoption. Neither Amanda, nor I, may discuss with anyone, anything that concerns adoption or child placement. I cannot give you, or anyone, information about Amanda's whereabouts."

Tina read the woman's nametag and said, "Marge, I noticed you called Amanda by her first name. Are you a friend of hers?"

Marge smiled politely and replied, "I have known Amanda Rutledge for many years."

Tina asked, "Do you have coffee with her, or maybe go shopping, or possibly go to the movies with her?"

Marge frowned, thought a short moment, and then answered, "We enjoy playing cards, and on occasion, we'll watch a movie. However, as I told you, I will not divulge her whereabouts. Such information is private and privileged. I cannot, and will not, give out any relevant information about Amanda Rutledge, or for that matter, anything which pertains to adoptions."

Sarah put her hands on the desk. She pleaded, "Please, Marge, listen to me. My mother died in the tornados that destroyed Westfield." Sarah held the letters up. "While sorting through her things, I found these letters that say I was adopted. No one ever told me about the adoption. My dad died years ago, so now, I have nowhere to turn. I have many questions. I would truly like to know some answers. Will you please help me?"

Marge stood her ground. "The adoption process is a very secretive one. Ohio law binds me, and forbids me from giving any information. If I break that code of silence, I could face real penalties, or I might lose my job, or, I could even be imprisoned for such a violation."

Sarah pleaded again. "Amanda had to have known my real parents. I'd bet that she held me in her arms when I was only a small baby.

After all these years, I want to know where I came from, and who my real parents are.

Wouldn't you want to know where you were born? Please help me . . . pretty please?"

Marge took a deep breath. She paused, and then said, "I can't, Sweetheart. I'm so sorry, but the law is the law. I think you are a nice person, but I cannot risk breaking my oath of silence. You will have to go now."

Sarah sighed.

Tina stepped forward and tried her hand at convincing the steadfast Marge to help. She squatted down and put her arms on the desk. She looked in Marge's eyes and lamented, "Sarah has been through so much; the tornados, her mom's death, her destroyed home, and then, the last straw on the camel's back, the shocking news of being an adopted child. All these things happened to her in little more than a week. Her world is crashing down around her. Surely you could find some compassion in your heart for her?"

Marge frowned at Tina. She looked at Sarah, and said sternly, "You must leave. We have nothing further to discuss."

Sarah and Tina turned away.

Sarah shook her head in disbelief. "I can't believe this." She was so disappointed. Tears rolled down her cheeks.

Tina hugged Sarah. "Maybe we need to see someone else." She suggested, "Let's go back to Jan's and have another cup of coffee. Maybe we can figure out what our next step will be."

Marge watched the girls walk away. The phone rang, and she answered it.

Tina and Sarah returned to the café. They found an empty table.

Tina poked Sarah's arm and said, "We do know a little something."

Sarah wasn't sure what Tina meant. She asked, "What do we know?"

Tina smiled and whispered, "I am certain that Amanda Rutledge is alive. She couldn't be watching movies or playing cards with Marge if she wasn't. I'd bet that Amanda lives near-by, too. I doubt that Marge would be driving too far just to play cards, or watch a movie."

Wendy brought more coffee.

Sarah sipped her coffee before saying, "Yes, you are right. However, we have no clue where she might be. In reality, Amanda could be sipping on margaritas in Cancun, or, for all we know, drinking piña coladas on a sandy beach in Miami."

Tina shook her head. "I don't think so."

They lounged and discussed their options. They debated about hiring a private investigator. They talked about attorneys and lawyers, and even politicians they both knew. They were so engrossed in their conversation that neither of them noticed when a woman sat down at their table. Sarah looked when the woman tapped her on the shoulder. Sarah exclaimed, "Marge!"

Marge quickly put her hand over Sarah's mouth. She whispered, "Shh." She said very softly, "I am on my lunch break." She leaned between Sarah and Tina and continued. "I have a very good friend whom you would like to find. If I were trying to locate her, I would put on my thinking cap. I would also understand that I might find her name and address in a phone directory.

Here's something else you should know. Amanda, um, I mean, our friend, not unlike me, always wanted to live in Hawaii, but could never afford it. She also had a dream of moving to Florida when she retired. However, to the best of my knowledge, our friend has always lived in the Columbus suburbs. It seems as though it was Carthage, but I am not certain."

Marge slapped the table lightly with her palms, stood up, and hurried out the door.

Dumbfounded, Tina and Sarah stared at each other.

Tina called for Wendy. "Is there a city or town named Carthage near here?"

Wendy answered, "Yes, if you take 30th street, it will take you to the south edge of Carthage. It's maybe six miles from here."

Tina paid Wendy for their coffee. "Thank you so much!"

Tina and Sarah hurried to the car. Tina started the engine. Sarah clapped her hands and looked up. "Thank you Marge. You are a blessing from heaven."

Sarah found Amanda's name in the Carthage phone book. Tina drove to the address.

The large Victorian style home was in a well-kept neighborhood. Sarah noticed the wooden porch. "Isn't this gorgeous?" They stepped up to the door. Sarah touched her chest and admitted, "My heart is racing. I'm so nervous." Her hand shook noticeably as she rang the doorbell. Tina gently patted Sarah's back.

The inner door opened, and a petite elderly woman pushed open the screen door. She looked at Tina and said, "Come in, Sarah."

Tina's jaw dropped. She pointed at Sarah and said, "No ma'am, she is Sarah; I am Tina. How did you know Sarah's name?"

The woman snickered, "A little birdie told me you were coming. That poor little birdie, always wanted to live in Hawaii.

Bless her heart."

Sarah asked, "Are you Amanda Rutledge?"

Amanda confirmed, "Yes, Child, I am Amanda K. Rutledge." She motioned them to enter. "Come in, come in, and please hurry, you're letting the flies in!"

Tina and Sarah stepped quickly in to the house. Amanda led them to the living room. She offered them a place to sit. Sarah sat down, but Tina remained standing.

Amanda said, "Marge told me that you have a letter with my name on it. May I see it, please?"

Sarah handed Amanda the letters.

Amanda read them. She held up one of the letters and asked, "May I make a copy of this one? I will give the original back to you."

Sarah nodded yes.

Amanda left the room. Sarah heard a copy machine go through its printing cycle.

Amanda returned and handed the original letter back to Sarah. She held up her copy and said, "This is all I need."

Sarah asked, "Then you can tell me who my real parents are?"

Amanda said abruptly, "Oh no, Child, I cannot tell you."

Tina made a smart remark, "Oath of silence, right?"

Amanda scowled at Tina and scolded, "Patience is a virtue. Apparently, My Dear, you've not learned that most valuable lesson!

Bless your heart."

Tina apologized. "I'm sorry Mrs. Rutledge."

Amanda nodded her head. "Apology accepted.

Now, Children, I cannot tell you anything because I do not have the memory of an elephant. The date on this letter is August 23, 1987. I need some time to investigate. However, I will not promise you that I can find any information. Many of my good friends and connections have passed away.

Bless their hearts."

Amanda looked at Sarah and replied, "I am certain I held you when you were a baby. I held nearly all the babies.

My goodness, you are now grown, and I might add, very beautiful, too!"

Sarah blushed, bowed her head slightly, and said, "Thank you, Mrs. Rutledge."

Amanda made a hand gesture towards Sarah and smirked. "Call me Amanda." She waggled her head. "Hearing someone call me, Mrs. Rutledge, makes it sound like I am . . . well . . . OLD!"

Amanda sat down in a cushioned chair. "The adoption process is a quirky thing. Years ago, I swore to an oath of silence.

Silence, I suppose, because for many young mothers, it's a shameful thing to give up their child.

Silence, too, because it is a dreadful thing when a woman has such a yearning to become a mother, but cannot get pregnant and bear a child."

She smiled solemnly, and then shook her head. "I guess it all works itself out in the end. The adopted child finds a mother, and the new mother finds a child. The one left out though, is the despondent one who gave up a part of her very soul." She leaned forward and smiled grimly at Tina. She quickly looked at Sarah and asked, "Could either of you do that?"

Amanda's question caught them off-guard. They stared at each other with blank faces. Neither of them said anything.

Amanda sat back in her chair again. She put a hand on her cheek and continued. "I've seen joy, and I've seen sadness.

I've seen fear, and I've seen courage."

She pointed her hand at Sarah. "You are one of a very few of the adopted babies I've been able to see beyond their first birthday. It's not because I didn't want to; the adoption process simply disallowed it."

She paused in thought, and then rose to her feet. She politely corralled Tina and Sarah towards the door. "I will help you if I can." She picked up a pad of paper and a pen. She handed them to Sarah and requested, "Please, give me your phone number. When I find information of value, I will call you."

Sarah wrote down the number.

They hugged Amanda and said their good byes.

Sarah held Amanda's hand and said, "Thank you so much. You are such a blessing in my life."

Amanda smiled and caressed Sarah's cheek. "You go now, Child, I will be in touch.

Bless your heart."

Tina and Sarah left Carthage and headed back to Westfield. There was no conversation, so Tina turned the radio on.

After a few minutes, Sarah looked at Tina, and without saying a single word, reached over and turned off the radio.

Tina gave an understanding nod. She smiled at Sarah, looked at the road ahead, and said nothing.

Sarah nestled back in her seat, shut her eyes, and thought about what all had happened on this day.

She wondered, *"Is it fate?"*

Chapter Four
Meeting Dr. Sheffield

Sarah stopped her car on the street in front of an office building. She compared the address to the one on the card she had received from Dr. Sheffield. It was correct. All she needed now was a place to park. She drove slowly as she searched. Her quest seemed futile. Suddenly, she squealed with delight. Someone had vacated a spot directly in front of the main entrance. With mild elation, she celebrated her victory. "Yes, it's my lucky day." She quickly parked in the empty space.

She looked at her watch as she scampered in to the building. She checked the business card again and then quickly slid it in to her hip pocket. She thought, *"Room 237 is probably on the second floor."* She paused in the foyer, but did not see an elevator. She said in frustration, "Damn," and hurried up the steps. She stopped at the top of the stairs to catch her breath. She noticed there was no flooring. She saw stains on the concrete, and thought, *"There must have been glue or something holding down the old carpet."* She also noticed there was no base trim, and that the walls were bare.

She saw a metal folding chair about halfway down the hall. There was a sign attached to the chair, but it was too far away to read. She walked towards the chair. The sounds of her hard-sole shoes tapping on the concrete floor echoed in the empty hallway. She thought, *"Someone must be remodeling."* She paused near the chair to read the hand written sign. *"Dr. Sheffield, 237."*

She looked at her watch and then crinkled her face. She scolded herself, "You're twenty minutes late." She took a deep breath, cringed slightly, and then opened the door. She peeked around the edge of the door and stepped quietly inside. She expected to see a secretary or possibly someone who might greet people when they entered the room. However, what she saw was an empty desk. In fact, things were not at all how she had envisioned them. She stopped and looked around. The door automatically closed behind her.

She found herself standing in a very large room with tall ceilings. There were several people, possibly as many as 12, seated on folding chairs, which formed a circle. All of them were staring at her. Standing in the middle of the circle was a dark-haired man. He was looking directly at her. He wore glasses, and sported a silvery frosted beard and mustache.

The man gave a kind smile and said, "Good afternoon."

Sarah replied, "I'm looking for a Dr. Sheffield."

The man answered, "I am Dr. Sheffield."

Sarah felt embarrassed. She apologized, "Please forgive my being late. I will go. I will reschedule."

Gesturing with both hands, Dr. Sheffield exclaimed, "No, no, you come right on in."

Sarah didn't budge. "Um, no thank you. This is not what I expected. I'll go. Have a nice afternoon." She quickly turned and stepped toward the door.

Dr. Sheffield spoke loudly, "Sarah, if you leave now, you may never find the answers to your questions."

She turned to face him. She asked curiously, "How do you know my name?"

He chuckled, held up a sheet of paper, and revealed, "Everyone on this list is here except a person named Sarah. I presumed you were Sarah. Was I correct?"

Sarah tilted her head and rolled her eyes. She shrugged her shoulders and nodded. "Yes, I am Sarah Meeks."

Dr. Sheffield said, "I apologize that this office is in an unfinished state. The bleakness does take away from the atmosphere. However, if you perceive this as a group session, I assure you, this arrangement is merely a temporary one.

As you can see, Sarah, there are two available seats. You have three options." He pointed to a chair, which was in the middle of the circle. "One, you can sit here, where you will be the center of attention, and I will direct my efforts towards you, specifically." He pointed to a second chair. "Two, you can sit in the empty chair which is a part of the circle. There, you will join the others

49

by being a part of the discussion. You may share your thoughts and questions, and I will direct my efforts towards you and the others, collectively."

He pointed behind Sarah. "Or, you may choose option three, which is to leave. If you choose to leave, you risk never achieving your first goal, which is to have your questions answered.

We are all here for the same reason. You, and those sitting here, wish to understand Out of Body Experiences."

He raised his hand, palm up and asked, "Is an Out of Body Experience real, or, is it a figment of your imagination? Are Out of Body Experiences simply silly dreams?

You may stay or leave, the choice is yours."

Sarah stared with uncertainty. She quickly spun, turned the doorknob, and pushed the door open.

Dr. Sheffield warned, "Stop! If you leave, you may never know!"

The door tried to close automatically, but Sarah reached out and held it open. She thought for a moment, and then lowered her head. She let the door shut completely, and turned back toward Dr. Sheffield. She reached back and grabbed the doorknob again. She asked, "How do I know you are who you say you are, and whether or not you have answers to my questions, some of which I haven't even asked?"

He calmly answered, "If you do not believe the things I will tell you, then, your search for answers will be wasted on this day and this moment only. If you leave, your search may never end.

At this point, you can join me and listen to my answers, hoping to understand, or you may leave and continue your quest elsewhere."

He raised his hands and assured, "I charge no fee, so please, join me."

Sarah looked at the circle of people and then at Dr. Sheffield. She let go of the doorknob and walked over to them. All eyes were on Sarah. Reluctantly, she chose to sit in the middle of the circle.

Dr. Sheffield smiled. "Very good, Sarah, you have demonstrated your willingness to face your fears and curiosities and share them with the others."

Sarah took a very deep breath and then exhaled loudly. "Yes, I suppose so."

Dr. Sheffield began by handing out clipboards with paper and pens. "I will now address the first two questions Sarah asked a minute ago. Who am I, and how does she know that I have the qualifications to answer her questions about Out of Body Experiences?

I am, indeed, a doctor, as my name implies. I have studied at Chicago University, Stanford University, and The University of Nevada-Las Vegas. I majored in Psychology, and Bodily Sciences at Stanford; Neurology and Brain Research at Chicago; and for some unknown reason, Political Science at UNLV. I am now a professor at Miami of Ohio University, where I teach Psychology and Home Economics."

Sarah and a few of the others chuckled.

Dr. Sheffield smiled and quipped, "I am kidding about the Home Economics. If you could see my apartment, you would understand why I do NOT teach it.

I became interested in Out of Body Experiences when I began having them myself. I have spent the past 7 years studying them. I am writing a book about Out of Body Experiences. I hope to prove what causes them to occur. If the contractors ever get my office renovation done, I will display my certificates for your examination. If any of you feel I am not qualified to speak here this afternoon, you are at liberty to leave." He paused.

Nobody left.

"Good, you have all chosen to stay. I shall continue.

Today, I will give you a brief overview about Out of Body Experiences. I am sure there will be many more questions than I can possibly answer in our allotted time. Please take notes and write your questions down. I will address each of your personal questions during future individual private meetings."

Dr. Sheffield moved to a place where he could address them as a group. He continued. "Most of you are here because you want to know what an Out of Body Experience is." He shrugged slightly. "Some people call them dreams while others call them visions, or illusions." He grabbed his chin, tilted his head, and admitted, "It is quite possible that some of you knew what to call them before you came here."

He raised his index finger. "Let me begin by mentioning that I have received and read the preliminary information forms that each of you returned to me. I have determined from the information contained in those reports, that all of you are here because you've had one or more Out of body Experiences." He nodded as he scanned the group. "However, my research and studies lead me to say that even though you may not admit it, most of you have had at least 6 of them, if not as many as a dozen. You likely brushed off the first one or two events as silly dreams. Numbers 3 and 4 scared you because you thought you might be losing your mind. Five and six brought on curiosity, and the desire to know what's going on. For those of you who have had more than six, you've been trying to figure out how or why they happen.

It is possible, that some of you may have learned how to control your movement during an Out of Body Experience."

He paced slowly as he spoke further. "Allow me to return to the original question, which was; what is an Out of Body Experience?"

All eyes were on Dr. Sheffield.

He held up an open hand and said, "But first, I feel it is important to tell you what an Out of Body Experience, is NOT!

He stopped pacing and faced the group. He emphasized each of his statements with a hand gesture. "An out of Body Experience is not a dream, nor is it a nightmare.

An Out of Body Experience is not a physical or mental abnormality.

Even though an Out of Body Experience may seem like a form of telepathy or extra sensory perception, umm, ESP, if you will, it is not. Telepathy and ESP pertains to the passing of information from one person or brain to that of another person or brain. In those settings, the information is transferred without the use of audible, visual, or touching sensations."

He stepped to the middle of them and looked at the circle of faces.

He paused, clasped his hands together, and smiled slightly. He stated, "An Out of Body Experience is not the last thing that happens before you die."

He left the circle once again, and spoke to them as a group. "In conclusion, what should be further understood is that an Out of Body Experience is not a religious type of spiritual revelation, nor is it an apparitional intervention."

He paused, raised both hands slightly, and then scanned the circle.

He clasped his hands again. "Now that we know what an Out of body Experience is not, I will move on with pertinent information about what they ARE."

He touched his head as he spoke. "An Out of Body Experience is usually associated with deep meditation or the altering of the brain to the point of being comatose."

He waved his hand. "Patients who are being treated in the intensive care unit of a hospital will sometimes report having an Out of Body Experience. Generally, they've been heavily sedated which can certainly make that possible. A person in the hospital will sometimes talk about having a Near-Death Experience. A Near-Death Experience and an Out of Body Experience are one in the same. The word, death, merely dramatizes the event. I suppose that saying the word death makes an Out of body Experience sound more glamorous or something."

He grinned, and nodded as he stated, "Yes, for those of you who might be wondering, a drinking binge, or a near drug overdose can trigger an Out of Body Experience."

He waited for those who were taking notes to catch up.

"I will now talk about what happens during an Out of Body Experience.

He raised his forefinger. "Let me use an uncomplicated example that is not affected by emotions or dramatization."

He stepped closer to Sarah and placed his hand on her shoulder. "Let's assume that Sarah is at home and sitting in her living room. Let's also assume that she wants to enjoy being out on her porch.

In order for her to experience being on the porch, she will have to stand up, walk over to the door, open the door, and step outside. When she arrives on the porch, she will be able to feel the cool breeze on her skin, smell the fresh air, and hear the wind in the trees. In other words, she will physically perform the tasks required to go out on the porch and experience it. She will have expended time and energy to achieve her notion. By using her senses, she will be able to enjoy the porch. If she chooses to be somewhere else, she must expend more time and more energy to do so. Her body and her spirit move as one because her spirit has never been separated from her body or the physical world."

He paced slowly and, once again, emphasized. "Your spirit has no physical properties. You cannot see it, touch it, hear it, smell it, or taste it.

Your spirit is not a part of the physical world. Nonetheless, your preconceived ideas about your spirit have placed limitations on it, which, in turn, have kept it locked inside your body. However, your misconceptions do not have it imprisoned there.

Your spirit is a part of you, which your thoughts or your notions can control. You can move it out of your body simply by using your thoughts to tell it where to go.

Conversely, when a spirit is, umm, let me say, disconnected, as in the case of an Out of Body Experience, it will send sensations back to your living being. You will feel, see, smell, hear, and taste, and so on. Further, you will know emotions. You will feel and understand love, joy, despair, sadness, and pain. Everything you can feel or sense, the disembodied spirit can transmit back to your mind.

If Sarah wants to experience going out on the porch, but is too tired to up and do so, she can still enjoy her notion.

She's been on the porch hundreds of times. She remembers the parts of her experience that she enjoys the most. She recalls the sounds of the birds, or the smell of freshly cut grass. Without leaving her chair, she could close her eyes and cause her spirit to go out on the porch. She'd remain perfectly still, but, by means of her disembodied spirit, would be able to feel the wind on her face. She could feel the roughness of the wooden railing when she leans against it to see the clear blue sky."

He paused, and made eye contact with some of the group, including Sarah.

"I can tell that I am confusing some of you. You're probably thinking that an Out of Body

Experience is nothing more than a trip down memory lane. Your thought would be true for the most basic form of an Out of Body Experience. However, higher levels of Out of Body Experiences will take you beyond the memories you have stored in your mind. During an Out of Body Experience, you can revisit any time or place associated with your life. Where your memory, in some way, might lose or obscure some of the details of an event, an Out of Body Experience will not. While an Out of body Experience will put you at the same time and place that you've remembered, the difference will be your ability to relive the selected experience completely unobscured. In doing so, you will rediscover certain things about the particular time and place that may have long since been forgotten."

He gave an inquisitive smile. "Some of you are thinking, time travel.

It is time travel, but in the sense where you can only travel to times and places which pertains to you personally. In other words, Sarah could not have an Out of Body Experience and go to somewhere in MY life."

He looked at Sarah, paused, raised his index finger, and said, "Wait, let me clarify my statement. Sarah could experience something in my life if what she wants to experience involved both her and me. She could not, however, experience events that were specific to my life only."

He clasped his hands together. "In conclusion, an Out of Body Experience, IS, a walk down memory lane.

It IS a trek through time."

He released his hands. "Although these experiences are not of the physical world, you will certainly excite your senses as though you are right there living them. By learning how to control your Out of Body Experience, you can, and will, enjoy life with a whole new perspective."

He placed his palms together. "I am sure that each of you has many questions. I want to answer all of them, but I must protect the personal privacy of each of you. Therefore, at this time, I will not continue this discussion and expose your personal lives or information in this group atmosphere."

He raised his hands, smiled, and admitted, "I did something of which none of you are aware. When you opened the envelope that I mailed to you a few weeks ago, you should have found information about this session. You should have also found a business card with my name, address, and phone number on it."

Some of the group nodded and pulled a card from their pocket.

Dr. Sheffield said with confidence, "I attached a psychic suggestion to each of your cards. When you touched the card, you would remember to bring it with you to this meeting."

He pulled a small stack of business cards from his pocket. "I have some extra cards if any of you do not have yours." He held the cards in the air above his head.

The room fell eerily silent.

Nobody requested a card.

He grinned and said, "I didn't think so." He put the cards back in his pocket.

He instructed, "In two weeks, I hope that my office renovation will be complete. Please call and schedule your next session with me after then."

Sarah pushed her hand in to her hip pocket and pulled out Dr. Sheffield's card.

In awe, each person in the circle looked at his or her card. Those with blank stares seemed to ask without saying, *"How could he have accomplished this?"*

Sarah looked up when she heard the office door shut.

Without notice, Dr. Sheffield had left.

Chapter Five
Beyond the Circle

Two weeks to the day, Sarah called to make another appointment. She was anxious to learn more about Out of Body Experiences.

She returned to Dr. Sheffield's office. His newly completed office impressed her. The carpet was beautiful, and the paintings on the walls were formal. The leather furniture and matching decor gave the room a fall-like feeling. However, the biggest change was the ceiling. First, it was not as high as before. Second, the textured tiles gave the room a sense of grandeur; and third, the lights gave off a peaceful glow. She felt comfortable in the somber atmosphere, especially with no people there to stare at her.

She went to Dr. Sheffield's personal office. She sat patiently at his desk and waited. His office was not large, but it had a homey feeling.

Dr. Sheffield came in the office. He sat in a large leather chair that was behind his desk. He began reviewing the subjects covered in the last meeting. She listened intently, and said nothing.

He finished the overview, and then leaned back in his chair. He asked, "I gather you have some questions?"

Sarah nodded as she took a note pad from her purse. "Yes I do, and I hope you will answer them for me."

He smiled, nodded at her, and said, "Proceed."

Sarah spoke with confidence. "I understand that during an Out of Body Experience my spirit is leaving my body and later returning. I also understand that my spirit can sense things and that my body will feel them as well. However, those things are what happen after an Out of Body Experience begins. I want to know what causes me to have an Out of Body Experience in the first place."

Dr. Sheffield responded by asking his own question. "Are you an only child?" Without allowing Sarah to answer, he continued. "It is a known trait for children with no siblings to experience a higher level of stress. They function quite normal in a social atmosphere, but there is stress lurking below the surface. This undetected level of stress can cause undue anxiety. Anxiety overrides certain emotional conditions and forces the mind into a state of involuntary sedation. When a person falls to sleep, this condition is more likely to incite an Out of Body Experience. To add to this, if a person drinks alcohol, or uses some type of drug to alter their mind in some way, the chance for an occurrence increases dramatically."

Sarah frowned, and answered sternly, "First of all, Dr. Sheffield, I do not abuse drugs of any kind. I am not, as you put it, interested in altering my mind. I do admit there were occasions when I may have consumed more alcohol than I should have, but I do not believe that overindulgence is a problem for me.

As for being an only child, yes I am. However, I recently discovered that I am an adopted child. My parents adopted me when I was only nine weeks old. I have always thought of my adoptive parents as my true mother and father. Furthermore, I was never told anything that would have led me to believe differently."

Dr. Sheffield jotted notes as Sarah talked.

She continued, "My mother died when the Westfield tornados destroyed her house. I found my adoption papers when I was cleaning out her home. I know this story sounds bizarre, but I assure you, I am not making it up."

He replied, "Tragic things do happen, and yes, they can indeed be bizarre."

She continued. "I've had many Out of Body Experiences. They started about a year ago. At first, I did not understand what they were. A few months ago, I began keeping track of them. To this date, I can remember having 17 of them. I'm having those more often, too. The most recent ones brought forth the reality of my mother's death. I thought that the shock of her death, combined with the news about the adoption, was pushing me over the edge. I thought I was going crazy!"

He assured, "No, Sarah, you are not going crazy. What is happening to you is common among those who wish to admit they are having Out of Body Experiences. Your added demise is encouraging your mind to let go of reality. Subconsciously, your mind is seeking a place of calm and serenity. Emotionally, you need a place with no turmoil. An Out of Body Experience can take you there. What you need to do is learn how to control what happens during your Out of Body Experience. You mentioned in your paperwork that you have learned to move your disembodied spirit from place to place. This is the very essence of an Out of Body Experience. Now, of course, you know that you can consciously control your spirit in many ways.

Tell me more."

Sarah paused in thought, and then cleared her throat to speak. "During my Out of Body Experiences, I will open my eyes and, usually, find myself floating above my bed. At first, this scared me, and I'd wake up immediately. Eventually though, I became accustomed to the phenomenon.

Somewhere along the way, I realized I could move around in the room by simply thinking about being somewhere else."

Dr. Sheffield continued taking notes.

Sarah talked on; "I became frustrated when I kept running into the wall. It didn't hurt or anything, but I felt it.

Two weeks ago, I made a great discovery. During an Out of Body Experience, I remembered what you said at the group session. All I needed to do was think about being somewhere, and I could go there by releasing my spirit to do so."

Sarah remembered, "It was a moonlit night. I was floating in my bedroom and looking out the window. It seemed so peaceful beyond the window. I deliberately thought, "I want to go outside." She put her hand on her cheek. "My God, my body, um, I mean spirit, floated right through the glass, and, all of a sudden, I was outside. It scared me, and I instantly returned to my body.

A few nights later, I did it again, only this time, after going through the window, I floated up to the treetops. I could feel the wind on my face. I could smell the fresh air. I was at peace with myself. I felt good. I was there for only a few minutes because I was afraid of being too far from my body. I returned and went no farther."

Without warning, Dr. Sheffield applauded. He exclaimed loudly, "Bravo!"

The sudden outburst startled Sarah, and she reared back in her chair.

He reached out his hand and apologized, "I am so sorry. I didn't mean to scare you."

He quickly explained, "You see, Sarah, when you passed through the window, you did so because your mind no longer perceived the window as a physical barrier. You have learned that your spirit has no deterrents. This is very important to remember, as it will further help you to comprehend your Out of Body Experiences. As you adjust to this newfound amenity, you will be able to expand your boundaries.

It pleases me to know that you have progressed so quickly. What you have accomplished might take other people years to carry out. Based on what you have described to me, I can say that you are on the threshold of something wonderful.

You mentioned the death of your mother. If you wish, all you need to do is think of a favorite time, and you could be with her again. Maybe it was your birthday party, or possibly Christmas. You can go as far back as your mind will allow. Don't be afraid. You can return to your body at any time by simply thinking it."

Sarah squirmed with excitement. "How do I make an Out of Body Experience happen?"

Dr. Sheffield answered, "Unfortunately, there is still no definitive way that I know of, that will cause an Out of Body Experience to occur. I am compiling information with hopes of proving that certain things will trigger or cause an Out of Body Experience to happen. That is why I charge no fees for anyone to consult with me. I will take the information you have provided and compare it with the information of many others.

So far, my research indicates that because every person is different, so too will each person's trigger mechanism be different. What triggers an

Out of Body Experience for some will differ from what might trigger one for you or me. Given time, I believe you will come to know what you need to do to cause an Out of Body Experience to occur. For now, you are at the mercy of your mind. Since you are now aware of why they occur, you can enjoy them."

He leaned forward and placed his arms on the desk. "I will ask that you please take notes about your everyday activities. By doing so, maybe we can discover what is triggering your Out of Body Experiences."

He stood up and concluded. "I do not need a minute by minute accounting of your days and nights. You might begin with keeping track of your sleeping schedule. You might also keep track of your alcohol consumption. Please, try not to change the way you do things. Rather, you need to allow your habits to help us discover what is affecting your mind, which in turn should reveal what might be causing your Out of Body Experiences.

You may contact me at any time. When, and if, you believe you have discovered something of value, please call. Try to remember what happens during your Out of Body Experience. Write it down, if you can. Do not worry if you cannot remember every detail. The mind will sometimes block certain events. Nonetheless, the more information you can accumulate, the better we can do with your knowledge and understanding.

There is no need for pre-arranged consultation. If you wish to talk with me, simply call for an appointment. I will be more than happy to accommodate your needs."

Sarah stood up. "Thank you so much for helping me. I will do all I can."

Sarah left Dr. Sheffield's office with a better feeling about Out of Body Experiences. She also understands how they influence her life.

She's excited to know that with a simple whim, she can return to the special times she shared with her mom and dad. She will, once again, enjoy those feelings of love, which, in the past, had tragically disoriented in her life.

Weeks passed and Sarah kept track of everything she could. Dr. Sheffield could not pinpoint an exact trigger mechanism for her Out of Body Experiences. However, he did narrow the probable cause to a few obvious things.

Her stress level seemed the most likely culprit. If she has a particularly bad or emotional day, then, that night, she is most likely going to have an Out of Body Experience. Couple the emotional distress with the effects of a few drinks, and she now has the right combination to trigger an Out of Body Experience.

A naïve Sarah was innocent to the perils of Out of Body Experiences. She assumed she could do as she pleased; after all, Dr. Sheffield gave no warnings.

Sarah missed her mother and the love they'd shared. With each successive Out of Body Experience, she expanded her boundaries. She drifted farther and farther back in time, reliving forgotten parts of her happy childhood. Her newfound liberty intoxicated her. The yearning for love drove her lust for more of the addicting out of Body Experiences. Her hopes and aspirations swelled as she tried to console her broken heart.

Nonetheless, there will come a day when Sarah's innocent indiscretions will indeed, challenge her fortitude.

Chapter Six
Bêtise

Tina invited Sarah to join her for a drink at the Paramount Pub. A few of their friends happened by and joined them. The impromptu party grew into a drunken laugh-fest.

Sarah enjoyed the company of her friends, but tonight, all she could think about was the meeting she'd had with Dr. Sheffield. The mental distraction made it difficult to stay in the flow of the party. She watched Tina and the others at the table. They were having so much fun.

Tina noticed Sarah's distant look. Privately, she asked, "Are you okay? You look bored or something."

Sarah gave a somber smile and admitted, "I'm sorry, my mind is in another world." She grabbed her purse, stood up, bent down, and whispered to Tina. "I don't want to spoil the party, so I think I'll head home."

Tina asked, "Do you want me to come with you; we can talk if you need me?"

Sarah answered, "No, no, you stay and enjoy yourself. I will be okay. My mind is racing. What I need is to be somewhere quiet." She put her hand on Tina's arm, smiled slightly, and suggested, "Home is where I should be." She nodded as she said, "We can party some other time."

Sarah turned and announced her impending departure. She gave her apologies, hugged her boisterous friends, waved good-bye to Tina, and graciously left the bar.

At Home, Sarah prepared a rum and Coke cocktail. She took a sip, then went to the living room and sat on the couch.

She tried to relax, but all she could think about was her Out of Body Experiences. During them, she's able to visit her childhood. She can relive those times of love, when life was fun. Her heart fluttered as she remembered some of her favorite childhood days. She remembered the time when she had learned a ballerina dance. She was a very proud little girl. Without hesitation, she boldly performed the dance for her mom and dad. It was a very special time. She earned a standing ovation, followed by hugs and kisses from her two-person audience.

During Out of Body Experiences, loneliness evades Sarah, which, in turn, fuels her desire for more.

She went to the kitchen to refresh her drink. Her whimsical thoughts continued. She wondered, *"Where might I go on my next out-of-body excursion?"*

She returned to the couch. *"There are so many times in my life from which to choose."* She rubbed her index finger around and around on the rim of her glass. She pondered the possibilities for a long while.

Suddenly, she sat straight up. She put the fingers of one hand over her mouth. She wiggled her glass with the other. Wide-eyed, she exclaimed, "Oh!"

She paused in deep thought. Sounds of the rattling ice prompted her to go to the kitchen for another drink. Mildly aggravated, she banged the glass down on the counter. Keeping one hand on the glass, and gesturing with the other, she spoke aloud, "If, during an Out of Body Experience I am able to go to anywhere in my past, then why couldn't I go to my future?" She paused in thought again, and then filled her empty glass. She picked up the refilled glass and held it against her lower lip. She tasted the drink with her tongue, but did not sip it. She said softly, "Yes, I could see what I will become. I will know my legacy. I can see who I will marry, or even if I will have children." She sipped her drink and continued her thoughts. She giggled girlishly when she realized an oddity. She said brazenly, "I will even know my children's names."

She went back to the couch. She swelled with excitement as the many possibilities flooded her mind. She thought, *"Hopefully, I will remember that during my next Out of Body Experience that I will go to see my future."*

She finished her drink and went to bed. Her mind swirled with thoughts of her new plan.

Eventually though, she was able to fall asleep.

She awoke a short while later. She found herself floating above the bed. There was no need to panic, as this was commonplace during an Out of Body Experience.

Like a fleeting fairy from a children's story, she whisked herself around the room. She soared out the window and hovered above the tops of the trees. She spun slowly, contemplating her next move. She recalled her thought of wanting to visit the time of her special dance.

After a short moment, she remembered her plan to learn her future. She murmured excitedly, "What should I do?" She thought, *"I have no idea what the future might hold. Unlike my past, where I know about things that have already happened, where could I go in my future, especially when it is . . . well, nonexistent?"*

Much time passed as she pondered the possibilities.

Suddenly, she donned a mystical smile, threw her arms out from her sides, and gave a quick spin. She had made her decision.

She cleared her mind, and with reserved elation, tried to concentrate on one thing only. She focused intensely.

She closed her eyes, took a deep breath, and in a bold voice demanded, "I WANT TO SEE MY FUTURE!"

She waited, but nothing happened.

She opened her eyes slowly. In the distance, she saw two lights shining. They perked her curiosity. Delicately, she headed towards the glow. She heard rumbling thunder. The sound reminded her of a late spring storm. The air was heavy. The wind blowing against her face was damp and chilly. Her skin felt clammy. Her heart pounded, and her mind felt numb.

Darkness shrouded everything. The only thing she could see was the light. She felt anxious, but was not afraid because all she had to do was think about returning to her body, and her journey would be over.

The light seemed to call to her. It was almost teasing her to come see. She approached with caution, wanting to know what was there.

Suddenly, she was in the light. She tried to move forward, but something kept her from doing so. In awe of the situation, she quit trying to move, and began scanning the surroundings. She could tell that she was floating above a road. Curiously, she searched for the source of the taunting glow. To her left, she saw a car off the side of the road. The rear of the car was down in the ditch. The headlights were beaming towards a gray and ominous sky. She looked down from where she was floating. She could see the reflection of her face in the back window of a second car. The car was sitting against a tree. She heard a hissing noise.

White smoke rose from beneath the hood. She looked to her left again.

She saw a young woman lying on the ground.

Sarah felt uneasy. She thought, *"This appears to be the scene of a terrible crash."*

She looked down again. This time she saw a dark-haired man lying on the road. He was face down in a large pool of blood. Her heart pounded even harder.

She looked again at the woman lying on the ground. Blood dripped from the woman's motionless body.

Sarah studied her and thought, *"That woman looks familiar."*

She suddenly realized who the woman was.

She screamed in horror, "Oh my God;

It's ME; that's MY body lying there!"

Lightning streaked across the sky, and thunder shook the air.

In a panic, she cried out, "This is the scene of my death! Oh my God, it can't be! Surely, I do not have to die this way?"

Wrapped in fear, she covered her eyes and desperately wished, "I want to go back to my body!

Please!

Please!

Let me go back to my body!"

Sarah rose up in her bed and let out a blood-curdling scream. She trembled uncontrollably. In disbelief, she continued her appeal, "No! No! No!"

She grasped her head. It felt as though her brain was about to explode. The sounds of her racing heart thrashed against her eardrums. She felt every throbbing pulse of blood coursing through the veins in her neck.

When she realized that she was back in her body again, the pain quickly subsided. She put her hands on her cheeks and cried, "Please, I don't want to know this!

This can't be happening!

My God, what have I done?"

Consumed with fear, she left the bed. The room felt icy cold, and the moist air chilled her to the bone. She pulled a blanket from the bed, draped it around her shuddering body, and whimpered, "Dear God, what have I done?"

In a state of panic, she ran to the couch, covered her head with the blanket, and squeezed her eyes shut. She wanted the terror to go away. "Please go away . . . please!" Nonetheless, there was no escaping the horrible images or the marauding fears. Tears streamed from her eyes. She cried out again, "I don't want to know this!"

She wept even louder when she remembered seeing her own body . . .

Lying there . . .

Motionless . . .

Lifeless!

She remembered the man who was lying on the ground . . . his face in the puddle of blood. Her voice trembled as she muttered, "He must have been dead, too."

She shook her head violently and cried out, "NO! NO! I am not supposed to know this!"

Reckless thoughts filled her mind. She asked loudly, "Dear God, what can I do? I'm so afraid. I'm so alone."

Desperately, she pleaded, "Please, Mom, can you hear me? Will you help me?"

Her panic grew, but her options were few. She looked at the clock. It was 5:35 in the morning. In a frantic state of mind, her only rational thought was to contact Dr. Sheffield. She said confidently, "I know he can help me." She thought, *"The time of day doesn't matter." She said,* "He must help me!"

Her hands shook so uncontrollably that she could barely punch the correct numbers on the phone.

The phone rang several times before Dr. Sheffield answered, "Hello?"

Sarah pleaded, "Dr. Sheffield. It's Sarah Meeks. I have to talk to you. Please, you must listen to me!"

He replied, "Settle down, Sarah. What is so important that you would call me at this time of day?"

Sarah whimpered, "Oh my God, I've had a terrible Out of Body Experience. I'm so scared."

Sarah spoke with a shattered voice, "I went to my future! My God, I saw my dead body!"

Dr. Sheffield raised his voice, "What; the future; dead?

Oh my, tell me where you live! I will be right there."

Sarah waited, but her anxiety grew stronger as the minutes passed. Visions of her fated future kept flashing through her mind. She cringed in anguish. Drastic for help, she implored, "Where are you Dr. Sheffield?"

When she heard a car, she raced to the window. She was relieved, and said, "Finally!" She still had the blanket wrapped around her when she ran to the door to let Dr. Sheffield in. She led him to the living room. She sat on the couch. He sat in a chair across from her.

She put her trembling hands over her face and cried, "I can't believe this happened to me." She squeezed the blanket with her hands. Tears flowed down her cheeks.

Dr. Sheffield said softly, "Calm down, Sarah, and talk to me."

Sarah blurted out, "I didn't know this would happen! I thought I would be able to see my future. I only wanted to know if I would ever be married, or if I would have children. My God, I didn't want to know anything about my death!"

Dr. Sheffield scooted out to the edge of his chair. He rested his elbows on his knees, clasped his hands together, and stared at her. He sat quietly for a short time, saying nothing. Sarah remained silent, waiting for him to speak.

Dr. Sheffield released his hands and scratched his chin. He raised his hand slightly and turned his palm toward Sarah. He spoke with concern. "You have done a very dangerous thing." He scratched his ear and then slowly shook his head. "You should not have done this." He wrung his hands and said, "You must tell me more." He put his hands on his knees.

Sarah thought, and then put her hands on her cheeks. She explained, "I only wanted to see my future." She held the blanket tight against her chest. She asked, "Why shouldn't I know my fate?" The innocent comment infuriated Dr. Sheffield. He snapped to his feet, pointed at her, and proclaimed loudly, "That is NOT for you to know!" He shook his head in anger. "You don't understand what fate is!"

The sudden display of ire perplexed Sarah.

He closed his lips tightly, and glared. The muscles in his jaws flexed noticeably. He closed his eyes and used his fingers to massage his forehead. He pointed his hand at Sarah and shook his head. He made a fist to emphasize, and stated, "In your naïve moment of uncertainty, you precariously evaded death!" He pounded his fist against the palm of his hand. "The fate of all humankind is to die." He pointed at Sarah again. "If you would have tried to see your fate, you would have died in your sleep." He waved his hand angrily. "By seeking your fate, your spirit would have left your body. It would have gone to a place beyond your ability to live. You would not have been able to return to your body because your spirit cannot communicate with a lifeless mind."

He paused and stared at Sarah.

He exclaimed, "Your physical being would have perished. Your soul would have become a disembodied spirit, devoid of substance! My God; you must never do this . . . ever again!"

Sarah tried to justify her actions. "I didn't want to know my last day. I only hoped to learn and understand my legacy." She placed her fingers on her chest and asked, "What will my destiny be?"

A perturbed Dr. Sheffield argued, "You can only create memorable events if you are alive. When you die, what people remember about you is a part of your legacy. As I've told you, the fate of all humanity is death. When you die, you will fulfill your destiny. What lives on afterward is your legacy."

Sarah paused for several minutes.

Dr. Sheffield went to a window and stared out.

Sarah broke the silence. "I know how I will die, but I do not know when or where."

Abruptly, he turned and asked, "And, what do you think you would, or even could do, if you did know?" He raised his hands, palm up, shrugged his shoulders, and then, in disgust, threw his hands out toward Sarah. He scowled and turned back to look out the window. He crossed his arms, and shook his head in disbelief.

She replied, "I understand that I must die. It's the same for you . . . for all humanity, as you have said. However, if I can find out when and where I am to die, maybe I can change the circumstances of my death." She leaned up and asked, "Must I die such a tragic death?"

He quickly glanced at her. His mouth gaped open. She thought he was going to say something. Instead, he merely tilted his head, closed his mouth, and kept silent. He frowned, turned back, and stared out the window again.

She implored, "I don't want to die that way."

She saw him pull a set of keys from his pocket. He stepped toward the door. Without looking at her, he said, "I need some time to think. I am going to my office. Will you come see me in a few hours?"

Sarah stood up and begged, "Please, don't go, I'll make some fresh coffee. Please?"

He opened the door and looked at her. "You will be fine. Come to my office this afternoon, and we will discuss this incident further."

Without saying another word, he left.

Sarah sat down, closed her eyes, and repeated, "My God, what have I done?"

Her body felt numb. This experience had rocked her soul to the very core of its existence.

She could only cry. Her anxiety soared.

She laid back on the couch and thought, *"It was only a few months ago that my life was the same as any other girl."*

She frowned and said woefully, "Then came the storm, and ever since, my life's been spinning out of control!

Dear God, please help me!"

She wondered, *"Is there much more I must take?"*

She cried out, "Will it ever end?"

Chapter Seven
It's Time to Know

Sarah was still on edge because of her horrific night. The phone rang, which startled her. She quickly answered it, "Hello?" She recognized the voice, "Dr. Sheffield, I was about to come your way."

He replied, "I've been waiting. It's important that we talk."

Sarah explained, "I'm sorry that I didn't leave sooner, but I lost track of time. After you left, I made some coffee and sat down to think. I tried to remember what I could about last night. I've written down everything that seemed important."

He praised, "Very good. Please, bring your notes with you. I will see you in a few minutes."

Sarah made a tiff. "I need a shower . . . and something to eat. I'll be there in about an hour."

He agreed. "That will be fine. I have an errand to run. I'll be in my office afterward.

Goodbye, for now." He hung up the phone.

Sarah hung up, and went to bathe. The soothing hot shower helped relax her tense body. She finally stopped trembling.

After her shower, she hurried to put on a pair of jeans and a top. She checked her looks in the dresser mirror, ran a brush through her hair, grabbed her car keys, and headed to the kitchen.

She fixed a quick sandwich, got a bottle of water from the refrigerator, found her purse, and hurried to her car.

She ate as she drove. She arrived at the office building, parked, scurried inside, and rushed up the stairs.

Dr. Sheffield greeted her with an anxious smile. He seemed nervous to her. She was immediately suspicious of his unusual demeanor. She carefully watched him, trying not to be obvious.

He turned quickly and whisked away toward his office. She followed and watched him, but, once again, she felt tense. She thought, *"Why is he being this way?"*

There was a chair next to the desk. She pulled it out and sat on the front edge of the seat. She continued to observe him.

He stood behind his desk with his hands on his hips. He scanned several piles of notes that were stacked neatly on top of it. He opened a drawer and plopped down in his chair. He grabbed a pen and began tapping on the desk with it. He stopped tapping and clutched the pen in his hand. "Please, start at the beginning and tell me everything you can about last night."

Sarah grabbed her shoulders and leaned back in her chair. She put her hands up to her face and rubbed her eyes. She asked, "Where Should I begin, from the time that I got home, or, from the actual time the Out of Body Experience began?" He encouraged, "You may begin with the Out of Body Experience." He rolled the pen between his palms. "Please, give me every detail you can remember." He began clicking the button on the end of the pen. He looked away to retrieve a pad of paper.

The clicking sound annoyed Sarah. She spied at him through her fingers. She slid her hand down and covered her mouth. She stared at the pen and cleared her throat. She took her hand away from her mouth, tilted her head, and frowned. She blinked twice as she looked at him, but chose to say nothing.

He stopped clicking the pen and began tapping on the desk with it. He looked up, gave a slight smile, and waited for Sarah to begin.

She took a deep breath, put her palms together, and leaned forward. She crossed her arms and rested the weight of her upper body on her lap. She exhaled, and then spoke. "As usual, I woke up floating above my bed. I flew around the room, went through the window, and soared to the treetops."

Dr. Sheffield scribbled notes.

She continued, "I began thinking about where I might go or what I might do. At first, I was ready to go back to the day when I performed a special ballerina dance for my mom and dad. However, before I did anything, I remembered about wanting to see my future. When thoughts of my future entered my mind, I felt a strange sense of anxiety. It was like a feeling of . . . umm, how should I say this, eerie anticipation, or, maybe a premonition?"

He asked, "If you sensed danger, why did you go on?"

Sarah held her hand up to stop his comments. She smiled politely, and then continued. "I was captivated by the desire to see my future. I remember floating and slowly spinning, wondering what words I might say that would allow me to go to my future." She shook her head slowly. "I was confused. I wasn't sure of what to do. I thought; how can I know where to go, when my future doesn't actually exist?"

He raised his pen, looking as though he wanted to say something. Rather, he clicked the pen several times and put the end of it between his teeth. He thought for a second, but said nothing. He jotted down a few words, smiled, and motioned with the pen for Sarah to continue.

She shrugged her shoulders. "I simply said to myself, "I want to see my future.

At that point, a bright glow caught my attention. It seemed as though the light was calling to me. I didn't feel threatened, so I moved closer and closer to the light. I heard the rumbling of thunder. Everything around me was in darkness. The air was chilly and damp, and my skin felt clammy."

He asked, "Did you see anything as you moved toward the light?"

She answered, "No. The light was bright, but it did not hurt my eyes to look at it."

He asked, "What color was the light?"

She paused.

She winced and tilted her head slightly. "It wasn't a particular color. It was more of a glow or a sort of beaming. It kept luring me closer and closer. Suddenly, I was in the light."

He asked, "Do you mean that you were physically in the light, or that the light was merely present?"

She paused again before answering. "Um, I was not actually "in" the beam of light. I was in the "glow" of the light." She looked in his eyes and said, "The light was not pointing at me, or towards me." She donned a puzzled look. "When I got to where the light was the brightest, I could go no farther. Something was keeping me from going on. It was like the phenomenon of two opposing magnets. If I tried to move forward, something resisted and kept me from doing so." She frowned, turned her hand palm up, and said curiously, "I heard distant thunder." She sat up in her chair. "I kept hearing a whistling or hissing sound. Something smelled hot or smoldering. I'd smelled the odor before, but couldn't place it. I was a little scared, but I stayed, knowing I could go back to my body whenever I wanted. Before I could figure out why I was unable to move, I realized I could see things around me."

Sarah sat back in her chair again. She put her hands together and touched her lips with her index fingers. She paused in thought, and then revealed, "I think I was on a road." She hesitated again. She nodded slightly. "I saw two lights beaming toward the sky. They must have been the lights I had seen in the distance. There was a car to my left. It was off the side of the road and down an embankment. The front wheels of the car were on the edge of the road. The headlights were on." She surmised, "They must have been the two lights I saw."

She paused once again.

She put her hands on her cheeks. "Then, oh my God, I saw a girl on the ground. She was lying on the road near the car. I was distracted from the girl when I realized that I was floating above another car. I looked down and could see my reflection in the back window. The car below me was resting against a tree."

Sarah had a realization. She took her hands away from her face and held them up slightly. "Wait! Now I know where the whistling and hissing noises were coming from. The cars must have wrecked or something. The car below me had steam rising from it. The hissing was coming from under the hood of the car. I could smell radiator fluid or something." She pointed at him. "Yes, that's the odor I couldn't remember. It was the smell of radiator fluid on a hot engine."

Dr. Sheffield had stopped taking notes and was listening intently.

She put her hands over her eyes. "My God, there was a man lying beside the car below me. He wasn't moving. I wasn't sure if he was dead."

He asked, "Can you describe the man?"

She exclaimed. "Oh my God, he was lying in a pool of blood!" She bit her lower lip. "Umm, he was a white man with dark-colored hair. His hair was black . . . I think. Umm, I couldn't see his face." She stood up, put her hands on the desk, and looked directly at Dr. Sheffield. "The girl lying on the ground was ME! I could see my face, plain as day." She looked in his eyes, and then stated with certainty, "I was dead!" She put her hand over her mouth, which muffled her next comment. "My nose was dripping with blood." She pinched her shirt and tugged on it. "The blood had soaked my shirt."

He said nothing.

She kept her eyes engaged with his and leaned closer. "I could see my face as clearly as I am seeing yours."

She turned abruptly and walked to the other end of the room. She crossed her arms and turned back to face him. "That's when I realized I was at the scene of my death!"

He scribbled more notes, and then asked, "Could you tell where the accident had happened?"

She kept her arms crossed and leaned back on the wall. She looked at the ceiling. Tears flowed down her cheeks. "I don't know. I was so scared. At that point, all I desperately wanted was to return to my body.

I woke up, back in my body, and back in my bed. My heart has never pounded so hard. I felt my brain pressing against my skull."

He sympathized, "It must have been a terrifying experience, but please, you must go back in your mind and try to remember every possible detail.

Do you have any clue as to what time of day it might have been?"

She answered tersely, "NO!"

He fired off another question, "Could you see anything which might show where you were?"

Sarah was getting angry. She answered gruffly, "I said, NO!"

He asked another question. "Was it winter or summer?"

She put her hands up. "I don't want to do this anymore. I'm leaving!"

He stood up. "No, we must continue. Please, you must tell me everything you can."

Sarah grabbed a chair and shoved it. The chair tumbled and struck the desk. She yelled, "You don't care about my death; all you want is more information for your damn book!"

He slammed his pen on the desk. "That's not true!" He pointed a stern finger at her. "If you want to learn from this Out of Body Experience, you must cooperate! I cannot help you if you do not wish to help yourself!

The first time I met you, you were skeptical about Out of Body Experiences. You were even less likely to trust me. Nonetheless, you have come to know that I would never do or say anything that would be harmful to your wellbeing. Furthermore, I have done nothing to you which would give you any reason to not trust me." He put his hands on his hips and glared at her.

He shook his head, held his hands palm up, and explained, "Yes, I am writing a book. However, my book is not for my personal gratification." He lowered his hands. "My book is for you, and other people like you, who wish to know about and understand Out of Body Experiences. I can only help those who are willing to learn. In your most precious time of need, you are lashing out at the very person who can, and will, help you the most.

I can see that you're terrified.

I can see you're confused.

I can tell you're angry."

He walked calmly to her. He gently held her face, looked in her eyes, and said, "I can help you. Together, we can figure this out." He closed his eyes and gently touched his forehead to hers.

There was a short moment of silence. He then hugged her.

Sarah put her arms between her chest and his. She didn't push him. Rather, she walked through his grasp and headed towards the door. "I need time to sort things out."

He put his palms together and pleaded, "Please, don't go. We can make great progress if you will only decide to help."

She opened the door. "No! I must go now. I will call you when I can tell you more."

Sarah rushed out of the office.

Dr. Sheffield raised his hand and shouted, "Stop!" His command fell on deaf ears!

Sarah walked quickly to her car. She opened the door, and then looked back at the building. She took a deep breath and held it. She shook her head slowly. She released her breath, got in the car, slammed the door, and sped away.

Chapter Eight
Afraid of Living

A week later, Sarah made another appointment.

She stormed in to Dr. Sheffield's office. She glared at him and demanded, "What have you done? Why did you do this?"

He began clicking his pen and asked, "What are you talking about?"

She grabbed the pen from his hand and said, "You know damn well what I'm talking about!" She threw the pen across the room. "You have stopped me from having Out of Body Experiences."

He said nothing.

Sarah turned to leave. She took a step or two before abruptly turning back to face him. She insisted, "Give me back my ability to have Out of Body Experiences!"

He stood up and grumbled, "No! There are certain perils associated with Out of Body Experiences, and I need to know that you understand them. Until then, I will not allow you to go on."

She fumed and yelled, "Damn you!"

He defended his position. "You have crossed the line of no return. You believe you can change your fate. I will be no part of your self-pacification."

She crossed her arms and said, "I've remembered more about my Out of Body Experience. I think the new information would be of interest. Give me back my ability, and I will tell you. If you do not, you will never know."

He laughed. "Do not bore me with your childish attempt at blackmail. You see, I hold the upper hand in this situation. You cannot have an Out of Body Experience until I release the psychic suggestion I placed on your mind. Therefore, I know you cannot harm yourself with your naïve and irresponsible actions, which, by the way, could cause your premature death."

She stepped forward and scorned. "But you see, Mister Sheffield, I already know my destiny. I already know the manner of my death. I may not know the time, or the place, but only I can go there to find the answers. Without my help, you are nothing more than a paltry detective without a case to solve." She scoffed. "Goodbye . . . Sherlock!"

Sarah turned, opened the door, and walked away.

He shouted, "Stop!"

She stopped, but did not turn to face him.

He coerced, "You must confide in me. If not, you will never find the answers on your own. You will live a nightmare. Not knowing when or where you are to die will haunt you the rest of your life, for however long that might be." He crossed his arms and said in a conniving voice, "Will your death be tomorrow?

Will it be a week?

It could be a year or more.

And, Sarah, where will you die?

You don't know the answers, nor do I! However, if we work together, we can, and will, resolve those questions. Until then, I refuse to allow you to take any further risks involving your fate."

She closed her eyes, took a deep breath, and let it out. She was furious, but knew he was right. She stood motionless, biting her lip as she thought.

Disgusted by the situation, she began nodding her head. In a sign of defeat, she raised her hands and turned to face him. "Okay, you're right. I'll tell you what I know."

She pressed her fingertips together. "I've had time to think." She rubbed the top of her head with both hands. "Like I said, I've remembered more things about that night."

He motioned her to come back to the office. He said, "I studied your notes and have come up with some interesting opinions."

Sarah frowned and walked briskly to his office. She stood in front of an empty chair and crossed her arms. She swayed back and forth, as she waited.

He shut the door and returned to his desk.

She refused to look directly at him.

He sorted through several layers of notes. He pulled one out, read it, and then smiled. "Yes, here it is."

Like a pouting child, Sarah plopped down on the chair. She sat on her hands, stared at the floor, and said nothing.

He turned to her and said, "You saw the headlights of a car off the road. This leads me to believe that the crash happened at night. You also said that everything else was dark around you, which seems to confirm the assumption of it being nighttime. You said you were hearing distant thunder. This leads me to believe that there must have been a storm. You said your skin felt cold and clammy. If so, the air was most likely cold and damp because of the rain."

Sarah sat up. "Yes, and I saw occasional lightning."

He picked up another sheet of paper and read it. He looked up from his note. "You said that you saw your reflection in the back glass of the car below you."

Sarah nodded.

He gave a puzzled look. "This is curious. During an Out of Body Experience, you are in spirit form. It is hard for me to believe that your spirit could be seen as a reflection." He set his note on the desk and explained. "Please forgive this eccentric analogy, but it's like the phenomenon about vampires." He smiled slightly. "A vampire cannot see his own image in a mirror because he is no longer of this world . . . not unlike an Out of Body Experience."

Sarah raised her eyebrows and slowly shook her head. She shrugged her shoulders and offered no explanation.

He pinched his chin. "I'll need to investigate this."

Sarah leaned forward and put her hands on her knees. "I agree with everything you've said." She leaned back again and put her palms together. "I have remembered a couple other things which are not mentioned in my notes."

He rearranged his paperwork as he listened to her.

She continued. "It was dark, and I kept hearing thunder in the distance. However, there was enough light for me to see things. Maybe the moon was shining through a break in the clouds . . . I'm not sure." She put her hands on her face. "The road was not paved, and I'm sure that it wasn't dirt. I think it was stone or gravel. The car off the road was gray. The car below me was off-white or maybe a light tan in color."

He interrupted, "Do you know what type of cars they were? Were they Chevy, or Ford or possibly some other make of vehicle?"

She shook her head no. "I don't remember seeing anything that showed what brand of cars they were. Nonetheless, I am certain that the vehicle down the embankment was a car and not a truck." She nodded. "The vehicle below me was an

SUV of some type and not a car. The SUV had a large back window, and I'm telling you, I saw my reflection in the glass." She stood up and stepped toward the desk. She reached back, pulled the chair closer, and sat down again. She said softly, "I remember seeing two signs." She spoke louder, "One was a warning sign. It had holes all through it, as if someone had shot it many times with bullets from a gun. There was a curved arrow on it, warning of a severe right turn. Someone had shot the other sign to smithereens, too. It was long and narrow. I could only read a few of the letters on it."

Dr. Sheffield grabbed a blank sheet of paper to jot down what she had to say.

She described the sign, "It was broken in the middle." She gestured with her left hand. "The left half, or first half, had some of the green paint peeled off." She dropped her hand and continued, "The right half was hanging down. Both halves of the sign were very dirty. A tree cast a shadow, which made the sign even more difficult to see. The left half had three legible letters. There was an "A," an "E," and an "N." Just past the "N" is where the sign was broken; it was nearly in two pieces. I could only make out two letters on the right half. There was an "I" and a "D." I am sure there were more letters, but most of the paint was missing, and the bullet holes made it impossible to decipher any of them." She complained, "I have racked my brain trying to figure out the words."

She frowned and rubbed her forehead. "I'm getting a headache. This is all the information I have. Do you mind if I go now? " She stood up, which caused the chair to scoot back.

He asked, "Before you go, may I ask you a couple more questions?"

Sarah frowned, plopped back down on the chair, and sighed. "Yes, I suppose, but only a couple."

He gave a nod of appreciation. "Thank you.

You said that you are certain that the girl on the ground was you. Did you recognize any of the clothing you were wearing?"

Sarah answered, "My clothes looked normal. They were everyday types of things I might wear, you know, jeans, and a top."

Sarah sat up and raised her index finger. "Wait, I remember; I wasn't wearing shoes."

He wrote a note about the shoes, and then continued. "Are you certain the man on the ground had black hair? Could it have been wet red hair or possibly dark brown hair, or maybe, soaked with blood?"

She answered quickly, "I am positive. The man's hair was black. He was wearing khaki colored pants and a green colored shirt. The shirt had yellow or tan pinstripes running through it."

She stood up again and moaned. "I must go now. My head is killing me."

Dr. Sheffield escorted her to the exit. He praised, "Thank you for coming. We made very good progress. I will take your new information and combine it with the other you gave me. Please call me if you remember anything else."

Sarah gave an appreciative smile and a nod. She said, "If you decipher any of this, please let me know?" She turned and walked away.

Dr. Sheffield returned to his chair. He picked up his pen, leaned back, and began tapping on the desk.

Sarah returned home. She took some medicine for her headache and lay down to rest.

Dr. Sheffield began studying the new information.

A few hours later, Sarah awoke. Her headache had eased. She wondered if Dr. Sheffield had discovered any more answers. She thought, *"If we can figure out where my death occurred, maybe I can avoid being there."* She put her hand over her mouth and wondered, *"But how will I know when it will happen?"*

She lamented, "Yes, Dr. Sheffield, until I do know, this will surely haunt me!" She tilted her head. "Then again, if I do find the answers, I'll be counting the days and the minutes . . . which, too, will drive me crazy!" She put her hands over her face and screamed at the top of her lungs. "Please God, don't make me live this!" She shut her eyes and prayed, "Please God!

Please, pretty please!"

Weeks passed, but Sarah heard nothing from Dr. Sheffield.

She called his office to make another appointment. A girl answered the phone and said politely, "Hello, this is Dr. Sheffield's office. How may I help you?"

Sarah replied, "My name is Sarah Meeks. I'd like an appointment."

The girl apologized. "I'm sorry, but Dr.

Sheffield is no longer available for consultation. He has accepted a job at Auburn University."

Sarah barked, "But I must speak with him on a matter of utmost urgency! Please, how may I contact him?"

The girl replied, "I am so sorry, Ms. Meeks, but he gave no contact information for me to relay to any of his clients. I suggest trying his cell phone."

Sarah was instantly angry. "Surely he would not have left town without letting me know?" She became even more infuriated when she remembered the psychological block Dr. Sheffield had placed on her. "I demand to know how I may contact Dr. Sheffield!"

The secretary asked politely, "Will you please not yell at me about something that is beyond my control?

Three days ago, Dr. Sheffield hired me to work in this office. I will be here for only two weeks. I am sorry if you have a desperate need to speak with Dr. Sheffield. Nonetheless, I can tell you, with all honesty, that he left no information concerning his move to Alabama. I am to tell anyone who calls that he will not be returning to Ohio any time soon."

Sarah could tell she was getting nowhere with the uninformed secretary. She apologized. "I am sorry. I spoke in haste. I should not have been angry with you about my predicament." Sarah pushed her fingers through her hair. "I can see that you do not understand my situation."

The secretary informed Sarah, "I should probably let you know that in one week I will have this phone disconnected. You should also know that I am to contact the property owners of this building and end the lease agreement between them and Dr. Sheffield. This office will become vacant at that time."

Sarah took a deep breath and let it out. "I am not sure what I should do. I'm confused. Why did he leave without giving prior notice?"

The girl offered no explanations. "I wish I could help you Ms. Meeks, but I was given no other information. Therefore, I cannot answer any further questions. I hope you find Dr. Sheffield, and can get your issue resolved with him.

Have a nice day.

Goodbye."

Sarah sighed and hung the phone up.

She searched her purse and found a business card with Dr. Sheffield's cell phone number on it. She dialed the number. The phone rang twice before a computer voice answered. "We're sorry, the number you are trying to reach is no longer available."

Sarah screamed mildly. "Damn it!" Referring to Dr. Sheffield, she implored, "How could you have done this to me!"

Sarah used every avenue she could think of to try to locate Dr. Sheffield. She contacted Auburn University. However, administration officials at the college would not release any information without prior authorization.

The empty searches were frustrating. She felt abandoned. She had no place left to search, and no one to help her. She had only one option. If she wanted to find more answers where it concerned her Out of Body Experience, she would have to do so on her own. Determined, she thought, *"Fate may bind me, but while I am alive, I can certainly try to change my destiny!"*

On many nights, Sarah sat alone and poured over her notes, hoping to remember or find something she may have missed. She was desperate for any clue that might be of value. She hoped, in some way, to change the circumstances of her death. Her intentions were to disrupt what she perceived to be the inevitable. Nonetheless, she had very little information to go on. She was uncertain of how to carry out such a plan.

She decided that certain things would need to change immediately. She decided not to date for a while, especially black-haired men. She will deviate from her usual wardrobe of jeans and tops. She thought, *"Maybe the casual look of skirts and sweaters."* When not in a skirt, she decided to wear sweat pants with possibly a jersey-style shirt, *"anything but jeans!"* She determined, "I will also need to get a different car; any color but gray!"

She scrutinized map after map, trying to figure out the name on the road sign. She felt helpless and lost.

One solemn night, she put her hands over her face and cried out, "This will haunt me to my dying day!

Damn you Dr. Sheffield!"

Weeks passed and Sarah's social life slowly stopped. She lived with deep fear and anxiety. She was obsessed with finding the answers.

She hopes to find them before her tragic demise comes to bear.

Her destiny looms.

Sarah had been up most of the night and was not expecting guests. However, it was a welcome sight when Tina stopped by for an unannounced visit.

Sarah was very happy to see Tina, and gave her an enormous hug. They sat in the living room and caught up on lost time. Tina mentioned, "You haven't been at the bar in a while. Are you sick? I hope you're not mad at me or something."

Sarah apologized, "No, no, I'm simply struggling with a few changes in my life." She shrugged. "And because of those, I've been keeping to myself.

Thank you for your concern, but I'm okay, and I feel fine."

Tina replied, "You had me worried, so I came to visit."

Sarah comforted, "I'm glad you did."

Tina put her fingers over her mouth and snickered. "Guess what?" She touched Sarah's knee. "I was down at the bar one night this week;

I think it was Thursday. Guess what I heard?"

Sarah listened, but said nothing.

Tina continued, "A little birdie told me that Joe, you know, The Hunk, has the hots for you. He wants to ask you out!"

Sarah laughed. "Oh, is that right? Umm, tell me, was it a little birdie that told you, or was it Joe himself who started this rumor?"

Tina frowned. "Darn, how did you know?"

Sarah rejected the notion. "Tell Joe for me, no thank you. Tell him that I'm not looking to date anyone."

Tina argued, "But Joe is so adorable. He's such a nice guy. I just love his curly black hair and those sexy brown eyes. Come on Sarah, Joe could be a good thing for you."

Sarah stood up and spoke in a terse voice, "No, I just told you, I am not interested! I agree that Joe is cute, but I have too many other things going on in my life to have any type of relationship! Thanks, but no thanks!"

Tina held her hands up slightly. "Gee, I'm sorry I said anything. Let's change the subject." The phone rang.

Chapter Nine
Amanda Tells All

Sarah answered the phone. "Hello?"

Tina sat quietly.

Sarah glanced at Tina, and then answered the person on the phone. "Yes, this is Sarah."

Tina saw Sarah's face light up with a smile.

Sarah said, "What a pleasant surprise."

She put her hand over the phone and whispered, "It's Amanda Rutledge."

Tina grinned, and with reserved excitement, quietly clapped her hands.

Sarah continued talking with Amanda. "How have you been? I thought you might have forgotten me."

Sarah kept her head still, but looked around the room as she listened. She nodded, and answered, "Yes, I can come tomorrow if you like." She listened again.

Amanda's request surprised her, and she exclaimed, "Today? Oh my, I suppose I can, if you think I must." She covered the phone again and asked Tina, "Can you go with me to Carthage? Amanda wants to see me; today."

Tina shrugged her shoulders and agreed. "Sure, I'm off work."

Sarah gave Tina the thumbs up sign and answered Amanda, "Yes, I'll be there around noon." Sarah concluded, "Thank you so much, Amanda, you are a Godsend. I will see you in a short while.

Good bye."

Tina waited for Sarah to speak.

Sarah pondered a moment and then said, "Amanda is very ill. Her family is admitting her to a nursing home for a few days.

She has found some very important information concerning my adoption. She wants to share it with me before she goes to the nursing home."

Tina worried, "Oh my. You said she's going to a nursing home. Is she ok?"

Sarah replied, "Amanda didn't say why she is sick, but she sounded very tired."

Sarah looked at her watch. "When can we leave?"

Tina shrugged. "I filled my gas tank this morning. We could leave now, if you want."

Sarah agreed. "Great. Let's go.

Since you paid for the gas, I'll buy lunch."

Tina pointed and responded with one word, "Deal!"

Tina drove without the radio on.

Sarah's mind was on what information Amanda might have. She stayed very quiet.

Tina broke the silence. "Is everything ok with you? You've been so distant lately."

Sarah, still in deep thought, didn't answer.

Tina swatted Sarah's arm and teased, "Earth to Sarah. Come in Sarah. It's your best friend, Tina, talking here!"

Sarah blinked several times and looked up. She smiled and apologized. "I'm sorry; I was thinking about Amanda, umm, and some other things."

Tina spoke with concern. "We've been friends forever, and I can tell when something is bothering you." She squeezed Sarah's hand. "You can confide in me."

Sarah gave a much different answer than what Tina expected. "I need to get a different color car."

Tina's jaw dropped. She jerked her head toward Sarah, gave a puzzled look, and chuckled. She held up a hand and exclaimed, "You're telling me that you're upset because you want a different color car? What the heck's wrong with the gray one you have now? It runs okay, doesn't it? Isn't it only a year old?"

Sarah put her hand on her mouth and laughed. She touched Tina's shoulder. "I'm sorry. What I said must have sounded silly."

Tina's eyes opened wide, and she nodded vigorously. "Duh . . . you think?"

Sarah admitted, "Look, I am not upset because of my car." She explained, "There are many new things happening in my life right now. They're coming at me from all sides. I would talk to you about them, but for now, I need to deal with my issues alone." She squeezed Tina's shoulder. "If I need someone to listen, you know I will come to you first."

Tina reached over and patted Sarah's arm. "Remember, I am your friend, and I will be all ears, any time you need me."

Sarah nodded, and with a smile, said, "Yes, you are a very good friend."

Sarah reached over and turned on the radio. "We need a little music."

Tina sensed that Sarah was trying to evade further conversation. She remained quiet the rest of the way to Carthage.

They arrived at Amanda's house.

Tina knocked on the door.

Amanda greeted them with a hug, and invited them in. She guided them to the dining room. She stopped and tapped her hand on a large box that was sitting on the table. She cleared her throat and then spoke in a raspy voice. "Last week, Marge came over and wrestled this big box out of the basement for me. You remember Marge, don't you?

Bless her heart."

She put her hand on her chest. "My goodness, I can hardly talk." She coughed mildly, cleared her throat again, and continued. "A few days ago, I went to my doctor because I wasn't feeling well. He says I have a touch of pneumonia in my lungs. It's made me very tired and weak. My health is waning. I suppose my age is catching up with me. My son wants me to go to a nursing home. He hopes it won't be for long.

Bless his heart."

She waved her hand in the air. "Listen to me, squawking over a little old chest cold."

She touched the box. "Anyway, at least I found the strength to search through this box." She smiled at Sarah and said, "I was thumbing through a stack of papers from this box, and, lo and behold, I found your original adoption papers."

Sarah beamed with delight. "Oh my, that is very good news."

Amanda walked across the room to a china cabinet. She opened a drawer and retrieved a folder. She turned and faced Sarah. "You might want to sit down."

Sarah sat in a chair. She accepted the folder and opened it.

Amanda stepped behind, and rested both hands on Sarah's shoulders. "Bless your heart." She pointed at the open folder. "I put the most important letter on top. You can read it first."

Sarah held the first letter and noticed, "This letter is from the Judicial Offices of the State of Ohio."

Amanda nodded.

Sarah read the letter aloud.

"Dear James and Jennifer Meeks,

This letter regards your request for an exception to the Rules of Adoption.

We have received and reviewed your application. Our records show that you wish to adopt twin babies..."

Sarah was slightly confused. She muttered, "Twins?"

Tina encouraged, "Come on, read the rest!"

Amanda hugged Sarah from behind. "Yes, Sarah, bless your heart, read on."

Sarah scanned ahead, reading without speaking. She gasped, and then whispered, "There were twin girls, Hannah Marie and Sarah Lynn!" She then blurted out, "Oh my God, I have a sister, and her name is Hannah!"

Tina squealed with delight. "That is so awesome!"

Amanda smiled boldly. "Bless your heart. Now, read on, Sweetheart."

Sarah trembled as she searched to find where she had stopped. "Umm ...which, at the time of your application, were available. However, and it is with the utmost professional courtesy, I must tell you that Hannah Marie is now in a foster home and is no longer available through the State of Ohio Adoption Program.

You have impeccable credentials, which certainly qualifies you as adoptive parents. If you wish, you may continue the adoption process for custody of Sarah Lynn. Your only other option is to wait for another set of twin babies to enter the Program.

Whereas, the birth of twins is rare in itself, having twins to become available for adoption is even less likely. Therefore, it is my opinion that the time of your wait to receive custody of twins could be a lengthy one.

If you wish to adopt Sarah Lynn, I will mail legal documents to you in a few days. Please complete all sections of all forms sent, and return them for my review.

Bear in mind that it will be a few weeks before you hear from me about any decision. This process will need your patience, as it is a very slow and deliberate one.

I hope you understand that foremost in our ambition is the well-being of every child. It is our goal to match all adoptive children with responsible parents in a good home.

I look forward to hearing from you.

With all due regards, I thank you,

Amanda K. Rutledge."

Sarah sat motionless and silent, trying to absorb the new information.

Tina squirmed with excitement. "This is so cool!"

Amanda stepped aside and reached in the box. She pulled out a handful of letters. She began handing them to Sarah, one at a time. With each one, she explained what the letter or document represented. She held up a special one. "This is your original birth certificate. Please note that it reveals your mother's name."

Sarah looked at the certificate. "Mother, Marsha A. Langley." She flipped the certificate over and scanned it. She turned it back, looked at Amanda, and commented, "It doesn't say who my dad is. I wonder why?"

Amanda answered, "It was not uncommon for a father to omit his name from documentation. When a baby is born, especially out-of-wedlock, many young men are afraid of the legal ramifications. Another reason might be that your mother did not tell your father about the baby, or, it could be that your mother did not want anyone to know who the father was."

Amanda handed Sarah a small stack of letters. "These three are the follow-up letters I mentioned in the first letter you read. They contain a bunch of legal mumbo jumbo that you can read later."

Sarah examined the letters, and then placed them in the folder.

Amanda reached in to the box and got another letter. She looked at Sarah and smiled broadly. Teasingly, she started to hand it to Sarah, but quickly pulled it back. She waved the letter back and forth. "This one will allow me to put a feather in my cap. Actually, Marge had a good hand in finding this one.

Bless her heart."

Amanda kept Sarah from taking the letter. She sat down at the table between Tina and Sarah. She boasted, "This is the most important piece of information you will need."

Sarah and Tina listened intently.

Amanda put her hand on Sarah's forearm. "As you know, of course, your adoptive parents are from here in Ohio. However, your real parents are from Indiana."

Amanda allowed Sarah to take the letter.

Amanda continued as Sarah unfolded the letter. "They lived in Eastern Indiana."

Sarah reviewed the letter. "My mother filled this out. It's the official adoption form. She names the father as being, Mr. Mark J. Bangston, New Castle, Indiana. Mom must have been from New Castle, too."

Amanda confirmed, "Yes. Your mother ran away from Indiana and came to Ohio. She gave birth to her babies in a Cincinnati hospital. While there, she decided to give up her daughters for adoption. The bad news is, all the hospital records are now gone. They were lost in a fire many years ago." Amanda took the form, turned it over, and handed it back to Sarah. "Read section C. It tells about Hannah."

Sarah scanned down to section C and read it. "Hannah Marie: adopted by, Vernon and Gloria Sharpton, Cincinnati Ohio."

Sarah looked at Amanda. "Do you believe Hannah is still in Cincinnati?"

Amanda said, "I am certain she is not." Sarah gave a puzzled look.

Amanda reached in the box once more and pulled out another letter. "Marge had this letter in her files. Vernon and Gloria requested permission to take Hannah out-of-state. You see, back then, it was Ohio law that if adoptive parents intended to move an adopted child to another state within two years of completing the adoption process, the Judicial Court must grant permission.

Marge, bless her heart, was a secretary for the judicial court. Secretly, she and I kept many files and documents, many of which were never intended for public access. This letter gives Vernon and Gloria permission to move to Indiana . . . specifically, Richmond." Amanda handed the letter to Sarah.

Sarah smiled. A tear flowed down her cheek. "What you and Marge have done is very special to me." She hugged Amanda.

Tina said, "I see a visit to Indiana is in our future."

Sarah hugged Tina and agreed, "Yes, most definitely. We need to make plans."

Amanda commented, "Tina, you are such a good friend.

Bless your heart."

Amanda admitted, "I am getting tired. I need to lie down for a bit.

Please keep in touch, and let me know what you find out in Indiana."

Sarah hugged Amanda again. "I sure will. Bless your heart."

Amanda asked, "Before you leave, will one of you do me a favor by carrying this heavy box to the basement? You can set it on the first table you come to. I will put it away from there."

Tina grabbed the box. Amanda opened the basement door and held it.

Tina returned from the basement. "All set, I put it on the far end."

Amanda patted Tina on the back and said in appreciation, "That will be fine. Thank you so much.

Bless your heart."

Sarah gathered the pile of paperwork and placed it in the folder.

She and Tina left.

Sarah and Tina enjoyed lunch. They read all of the documents Amanda had given them.

They returned to Westfield. Tina invited Sarah to have a drink or two at the Paramount Bar. They enjoyed the drinks and planned a trip to Indiana.

First, they will search for Sarah's real parents in New Castle. From there, they will go to Richmond, hoping to find Hannah.

Tina turned away to speak with a friend.

Sarah sipped her drink. She closed her eyes and silently prayed. *"Please God, help me find Hannah. I could use a little good news in my life."*

Chapter Ten
Hope and a Prayer

Tina and Sarah headed to Indiana. Tina had only two days before needing to report to work. Sarah had hoped for more time, but Tina was a welcome companion. She smiled at Tina and said, "I appreciate your coming with me."

Tina kept her eyes on the road and replied, "I know how important this is to you. I would have never let you down. I had to pull some strings, but here I am!"

Sarah paused in thought, and then said, "I hope we can find my real mom and dad, that is, if they are still in New Castle, or, for that matter, even in the state of Indiana."

Tina spoke confidently. "By golly, I'm ready to give it my best shot!"

Sarah nodded. "Yes, I am, too!"

Tina gently tapped Sarah's knee. "I was thinking. This is like doing detective work. In my opinion, what we need to do first is find the local library. Most libraries are a wealth of information about people and events in the community."

Sarah nodded.

Tina continued. "They should have public records of some sort, things like old newspapers or even school yearbooks. I assume, too, that they would have a ton of information stored in computer files."

Sarah said, "I agree. When we get there, let's find the library, and see what we can come up with."

For Sarah, the 3-hour drive to New Castle seemed like an eternity. When they arrived, she was happy, yet somewhat anxious. Tina stopped at a convenience store and asked for directions.

She drove to the local library.

They went inside. Sarah walked up to the information desk. A middle-aged woman said, "Hi, my name is Cathy. How may I help you today?"

Sarah reached out to shake hands. "My name is Sarah, and this is my good friend Tina."

Cathy listened carefully as Sarah talked about the adoptions.

Sarah finished by saying, "I am searching for information about my mother and father."

Cathy replied, "Your story is very interesting. However, I'm not sure that I can be of any help to you." She gave a confident smile and rubbed her palms together. "Nonetheless, we shall see." She plucked a pen from a cup sitting on the counter.

Sarah spoke. "I believe that on the day I was born, my mom was a teenager. I also have paperwork which leads me to believe she was originally from here in New Castle."

Cathy slid a notepad closer. "Okay, let's begin with some names."

Sarah leaned against the counter. "My mother's maiden name is Marsha A. Langley. My Dad's name is Mark J. Bangston."

Cathy looked up when Sarah said the name Bangston. "I know some Bangstons, and you said Mark?

Sarah said, "Yes, Mark J. Bangston. Do you know my dad?"

Cathy replied, "No, no, I wouldn't know your dad. The Bangston name caught my attention. The Bangston family is very wealthy. Their name goes way back."

Tina chimed in, "Sarah was born in 1987. We were thinking; if, at that time, her mom was a teenager, she would have likely been going to a high school here."

Cathy said, "Well, if that is so, things will be a lot easier. There is only one high school in New Castle."

Cathy stood up and walked down a long narrow aisle way. There were tall bookshelves on either side. "All of our yearbooks are kept down this way."

Sarah and Tina followed Cathy.

Cathy slowed down and began pointing. "Let me see, 1960, 1970, 1980, 81, 82 . . . oh, here it is, 1987." She opened the yearbook and searched through the pages. A moment later, she said, "I was hoping, but I don't see anyone with the name Marsha Langley listed."

Tina gently grabbed Cathy's arm. "Wait, if Sarah's mom got pregnant while still in school, she probably quit. Sarah was born in 1987, so I'd guess that her mom might have quit the year before."

Tina touched Sarah with the back of her hand. "Remember what Amanda said? Your mom left Indiana and went to Cincinnati."

Cathy nodded in agreement. "Let's try looking in the 1986, or even the 1985 yearbook."

Cathy pulled out the 1986 copy and handed it to Sarah. She handed the 1985 edition to Tina. They flipped through the pages.

Suddenly, Sarah exclaimed, "MY GOD! MARSHA A. LANGLEY!"

Tina and Cathy looked up.

Sarah touched the page. "She is beautiful."

Tina coached, "See if your dad is in there, too."

Sarah flipped through the pages. She shook her head and said, "Nope, no Mark Bangston."

Tina moaned, "Ah, too bad."

Cathy spoke up. "The Bangstons were a prominent family in this area. They may have sent Mark to a private school."

Cathy politely took the yearbook from Sarah. "I'll make a copy of this page so you will have a picture of your mother."

Sarah praised, "Thank you so much."

Cathy grinned and held up an index finger. "Let's not give up on your dad quite so easily. I have another avenue to pursue." She walked between Sarah and Tina and headed back up the aisle way. "Come with me. I'll look in my computer for Mark J. Bangston." She returned to the front desk. Tina and Sarah followed close behind.

Cathy made a copy of the yearbook page. She handed it to Sarah, and sat down at her computer to begin a new search. "Let's see what I can come up with in the computer archives."

While Cathy searched for information, Tina and Sarah looked at the picture of Marsha. Sarah noticed, "I look like her, don't you think?"

Tina agreed. "Yes, you have her hair and her eyes. You must have your dad's smile."

Cathy sighed and exclaimed, "Oh no!"

Sarah and Tina turned to see what Cathy had found.

Cathy pointed at the computer screen and spoke sadly. "Here is an article from the June 6th 1990 New Castle Gazette. It says; Mark J. Bangston, age 22, died in an accident. According to an investigation, Mark was speeding through New Castle Park and lost control of his motorcycle. He crashed into a tree."

Sarah and Tina sighed. Sarah said, "That is so sad."

Cathy held up a finger. "Let me check something else." She searched her computer again.

"Here it is." She looked at Sarah. "I found your dad's obituary."

Sarah asked, "Does it say anything about my mom?"

Cathy said, "I'm sorry, but your mother is not mentioned. Your dad's grave is in New Castle Cemetery."

Cathy checked to see if there was any information about Marsha Langley. She shook her head slowly and said, "I'm so sorry, but, I find nothing at all about your mom." She let go of the mouse and turned her hand palm up. "The reality is that there's no way to know where your mom might be now. If she ran away to Cincinnati, she probably stayed in that area. It would be impossible to track her down without knowing her married name, especially if she tried to hide her past because of the adoptions."

Sarah was sad. "Yes, you are probably right, and she may not even be alive. I'll never know I suppose."

Tina spoke up. "Wait, Sarah, I've done some calculating. Your mom is in the sophomore section of the 1986 yearbook. She was probably 16 years old, or maybe even 15, depending on her birthday. I'm thinking she would have been 16 years old because she would have needed her license to drive herself to Cincinnati. Your mom would now be 41 or 42 years old. I have to believe she is still alive. However, I agree with Cathy; finding where she is will be the real challenge."

Sarah said, "If we had more time, I would try to find her."

Cathy said, "Finding your mom, without much to go on, will be a monumental task at best. I wish you all the luck in finding her." She stood up. "I'm printing out a copy of the obituary for you."

Sarah said in appreciation, "Thank you so much, Cathy, you have been a great help."

Cathy gave a friendly smile. "You are quite welcome."

Tina asked Cathy, "How far is Richmond from here?"

Cathy answered, "It's about 43 miles." She pointed. "Go back to the third stop light and turn right. The road is not a highway, but it does go straight over to Richmond. As a matter of fact, the road goes right by New Castle Cemetery."

Tina consoled Sarah. "Maybe we can stop there and find your dad's grave."

Sarah said, "I've probably found out from here all I can about my parents. I need to see if I can find Hannah."

Sarah sighed, looked at Cathy, shrugged slightly, and said with disappointment, "I was hoping so much to find my mom and dad. I was hoping even more that I would find both of them alive. I suppose that God has a reason why I didn't."

Cathy hugged Sarah. "I hope you find your mom. I'm hoping, too, that she is alive and well."

Cathy waved as Sarah and Tina left. "Goodbye, and please drive carefully."

Tina and Sarah found the cemetery. Sarah walked down row after row of headstones. She stopped and pointed. She had found her father's grave. She looked back toward Tina, who was standing near the car. Tina raised her hand and acknowledged Sarah's discovery.

Tina decided to allow Sarah some privacy. She sat down in the car and turned on the radio.

Sarah stepped closer to the marble and granite marker. She gently touched it. Her mind rushed with emotion. She stepped back and looked at the headstone. She wondered how it might have been to know her real dad. She spoke softly, as if talking to him. "My mom is beautiful. You must have thought so too, because she turned your head as well. Together, the two of you shared a special feeling. You shared something else, too; something that allowed Hannah and me to exist. Your situation may not have been the best of circumstances, but I will not judge you harshly, nor will I hold anything against you because of what happened. You shared love with my mother, and she, in turn, loved you back. I may never know all the truth, but I have to believe that you and my mom conceived Hannah and I in a heartfelt moment of love. I wish so much that I could have known you."

Sarah was unsure of what else to say.

She closed her eyes, and a teardrop fell on the headstone.

She said a silent prayer.

When finished, she looked to the sky and said reverently, "Thank you, God, for giving me this moment."

Sarah rejoined Tina in the car.

Tina hugged Sarah and gave her a tissue for the tears. "I am so sad for you."

Sarah wiped her face. "Don't be sad, at least we found my dad." She sniffled. "We can go now."

Tina slowly drove away from the cemetery. She consoled. "Maybe we'll have better luck finding Hannah."

Sarah smiled slightly, and with guarded anticipation, said, "Yes, I hope so."

Chapter Eleven
Finding Hannah

Tina drove for about fifteen minutes. Suddenly, she pointed and said, "Look at all those beautiful flowers, and yard ornaments." She slowed down to read the sign. "Perkins Pottery Bench, fresh flowers, candles and ornaments, gift shop now open."

Tina asked, "Would you like to stop?"

Sarah crinkled her nose. "Not really, I'd rather go on to Richmond. I could use a bite to eat."

Tina agreed, "I'm hungry, too. Let's go on. Maybe there's a nice place to eat in the next town." She saw a sign that read, "Hagerstown 12 miles." She said, "If there's no restaurant in Hagerstown, I suppose we'll have to wait and eat in Richmond."

Sarah nodded in agreement.

After a few miles, Sarah reached over and turned on the radio. She looked out the window as she searched for a clear station. A road sign caught her attention. It read, "Rangeline Road." She found a good station, glanced at Tina, leaned back, and began listening to the music. She thought nothing more about the sign.

Tina drove slowly down the main street of Hagerstown. "Hmm, I'll be darned; I didn't see a single restaurant!"

Sarah raised her hand in disbelief. "I didn't see one either." She motioned in a forward direction. "Let's go on to Richmond."

Tina stopped at a traffic light. They heard a honk. They looked to see where it came from. A young man was hanging out the window of a white colored pick-up truck. He was waving frantically, and seemed adamant about getting their attention.

Sarah looked at Tina. "Do you know him?"

Tina shrugged her shoulders. "Nope, I don't know anyone in this part of Indiana." The light changed and Tina drove on.

Tina and Sarah found a nice restaurant in Richmond. They enjoyed a tender steak. During their meal, they discussed the plan to find Hannah. They agreed to start at the library, the same as they did in New Castle.

Hannah was transplanting flowers in to bigger clay pots. She looked up when she heard the front door open. "Hi, Steve, how's the landscape business going today?"

He gave her a puzzled look, paused, and checked his watch. He walked to the counter where Hannah was working. "Didn't I just see you a few minutes ago in Hagerstown? You were riding in a black Chevy. Some other girl was driving."

She chuckled. "No hun, I haven't gone anywhere. I've been here all day. Why do you ask?"

He scratched his head. "I must be losing it. I could swear that was you at the stoplight."

Hannah replied, "Nope, it wasn't me, Kiddo.

Do you want something to drink?"

He said, "I'll have a can of pop and a cup of ice please.

Wow, that girl sure did look like you!"

She said, "Whatever, but I'm telling you, Half-brain, it wasn't me."

He shook his head. "I guess not."

Steve went to the side door. He opened it a little, looked back at Hannah, and said, "I need a couple-three bags of your best topsoil."

She said, "No problem, help yourself." She asked, "Do you want me to add those to your account?"

He smiled and said, "That'll work.

Thanks for the pop.

I'll catch you later."

Hannah waved as he left the shop. "Yep, I'll see you later . . . Half-brain." She snickered.

Tina and Sarah found the Richmond library.

Sarah told her story to the girl at the front desk.

The girl politely directed them to the lower level. "Tammy will be able to help you."

They went down the stairs and found Tammy. Sarah repeated her story, but added, "I am trying to find Vernon and Gloria Sharpton. They have a daughter named Hannah."

Tammy said nothing as she typed the names in to her computer.

Sarah waited patiently.

Tammy scanned the screen. She smiled. "Here we go." She then grimaced, and blurted out, "Oh dear!"

Sarah asked, "What?"

Tammy pointed to her computer screen. "It says here that Vernon Sharpton died on May 9th of 2000."

Sarah lowered her head. "Here we go again!" She looked up and asked, "Does it say anything about Gloria or Hannah? Is there possibly an address or something?"

Tammy said, "Hold on, I'm checking for information about Gloria."

Tammy put her hands on her face. "Oh my God, Gloria died in a trailer fire. She perished on November 16, 2003. It does say that a daughter, Hannah Marie, age 16, survives. I'll check the newspaper archive for related stories." Tina gave Sarah a small hug.

Tammy spoke up, "I found an address, but it's for where the fire happened."

Tina took a pen from a cup on the counter. Tammy handed her a blank piece of paper.

Tammy read the information aloud, "The fire happened at 1623 West Rangeline Road, Hagerstown, Indiana."

Tina said, "Hannah might be living by herself."

Tammy opened a drawer and pulled out a phonebook. "If she's not married, then her name might be in the local directory. I'll take a quick look."

Tammy raised her head and looked toward Sarah. "You said, Hannah Sharpton, right?" Sarah nodded yes, but said nothing.

Tammy checked several different spellings but found nothing. "No, I'm sorry, but there's no Hannah Sharpton listed."

Sarah was very disappointed.

Tina spoke again, "Let's go to the address on Rangeline Road. Maybe we can talk to the neighbors and find out where Hannah might be."

Sarah agreed, "Yes." She remembered, and said, "I saw Rangeline Road when we were coming to Richmond."

Tammy confirmed, "Rangeline Road is 6 miles on the other side of Hagerstown. It's about 22 miles from here, back towards New Castle."

Tammy apologized, "I am so sorry that I couldn't be of better help."

Tina praised, "Oh no, Tammy, you have been very helpful. Sarah and I will go to this address. If we come up empty, we'll be back to see you again."

Tammy smiled. "I wish you luck."

Tina and Sarah left the library and headed back toward New Castle. They found Rangeline Road. Tina turned the car on to the country road. She drove slowly as she and Sarah read the names and numbers on the mailboxes.

Tina complained, "Wow, this road sure is a curvy one."

Sarah spouted off, "Duh, you dingbat, they probably named it Rangeline Road for a good reason. Wouldn't you think that a road going through the range would be hilly and curvy?"

Tina smirked and said in a snide voice, "Yes, Smarty Pants, I suppose so."

There was no mailbox with the number 1623 on it, but by the process of elimination, they found what they believed was the correct address. The property was a field of tall grass with a spattering of small gnarly trees. There was no houses close by.

Tina suggested, "Let's go back to that orchard we passed a few minutes ago. Maybe someone there can help us." She turned the car around and headed back.

She drove slowly in to the parking lot.

Sarah read the sign, "Jessup's Orchard. This is a nice place."

Tina nodded in agreement. She parked in front of the main building.

Bells on the door jangled as they entered.

An older man came out from a back room. He saw Sarah and said, "Hannah, it's good to see you."

Sarah raised her eyebrows, tilted her head slightly, and replied, "I'm sorry, Mister, but I am not Hannah. My name is Sarah. I am Hannah's twin sister."

The man's jaw dropped. He exclaimed, "Oh . . . my . . . goodness." He reached out to shake hands. "My name is Calvin; Calvin Jessup.

I have to apologize, Sweetheart, I've known Hannah since she was a small girl, but I never knew she had a sister . . . let alone, a TWIN sister."

Tina gave a friendly chuckle, and said, "I am sure Hannah doesn't know about Sarah either."

Calvin scratched his head. "This is amazing."

Sarah asked politely, "Can you help me? I am trying to find Hannah."

A dumbfounded Calvin pointed at a table with chairs around it. "Please, sit here and tell me more about you and Hannah.

Can I get you something to drink?"

Sarah and Tina sat down. Sarah said, "I'll have a coke."

Tina agreed, "Coke for me too, please."

He returned with the drinks, set them on the table, and joined them.

Sarah asked, "How do you know Hannah? Do you know where I can find her?"

Calvin smiled widely, and pointed. "Hannah lived across the road from here . . . um, that is, until Gloria, Hannah's mom, died in the fire. Hannah works for me part-time to earn extra money. And, do I know where she is? I sure do. I know exactly where she is." He put his palm on the table and said, "But first, I'd like to know more about you and Hannah." He raised his hand and promised, "Don't worry; she'll be at her shop until closing. She and her husband own Perkins Pottery Bench."

Tina chuckled, "Wow, we passed that place on our way from New Castle to Richmond."

He acknowledged, "Yes, The Pottery Bench is only eight miles from here."

Sarah sat with Calvin and told all that she knew about the adoptions and the real parents of her and Hannah. She also brought him up to date on the events that brought her and Tina to Indiana.

Calvin was flabbergasted. He listened to every word, but could only shake his head.

An hour later, he stood up and said, "This is absolutely amazing."

Sarah and Tina stood up. Sarah asked, "Can we go to Hannah now?"

Calvin donned a broad smile and replied, "We sure can. I'll drive, and you can follow me.

Say, would you do me a favor? When we get to the Pottery Bench, will you stay outside and allow me to bring Hannah out to you?"

His request seemed odd, but Sarah agreed. "I'm not sure why you would want to do that, but, yes, I suppose so."

He patted Sarah's shoulder. "Thank you.

Hannah will be so surprised. I can hardly wait to see the look on her face when she meets you."

Calvin drove his truck and Tina followed. He parked near the front door of the flower shop. Tina parked beside his truck. Sarah and Tina got out of the car.

Calvin said, "Wait here, I'll be right back with Hannah."

Hannah was sitting on a stool behind the counter. She stood up when Calvin walked in.

He said, "Hello, Hannah."

His unexpected visit surprised her, and she said, "I'll be darned, it's Calvin Jessup. I haven't seen you in a long time! How are you doing, My Good Friend?"

He replied, "I'm fine, but listen, Sweetheart, I have something very special to show you." He asked, "Do you have fifteen minutes? I need you to come outside with me."

Hannah was puzzled, but agreed. "Sure, I'm taking a little break anyway.

What did you do, Calvin, buy that new truck?"

He didn't answer her. Rather, he motioned her to come with him. She came from behind the counter and walked toward the door with him.

She stopped, grabbed his arm, and asked, "What's going on?"

He smiled. "You shall see." He put his arm around her and escorted her outside. He turned her so that her back faced the parking lot. He motioned from behind for Sarah to come.

Sarah tiptoed, and stopped only six feet away from Hannah. The urge to reach out and touch her was nearly impossible to resist. Tina could barely stand the suspense. She bobbed up and down with excitement. She bit her lip, trying hard not to make a sound. She had to put her hand over her mouth to keep from saying anything. Calvin slowly turned Hannah until she was able to see Sarah.

Sarah smiled. "Hello, Hannah."

Hannah was shocked. She put both hands on her face and cried out, "OH; oh, My God!"

She stepped back. All she could say was, "Oh, My God!"

Calvin said, "Hannah, this is your sister. Her name is Sarah."

Hannah shook her head slightly. She was speechless.

Sarah walked over to Hannah and hugged her.

Tina blurted out, "Yes! This is so cool! Damn, I wish I had my camera."

Hannah was unsure of what to say or do. She began to tremble, and nervously returned Sarah's hug.

Sarah said, "Hannah Marie, I am Sarah Lynn. I think we have a lot to talk about." She released her hug and stepped back.

Calvin could sense that Hannah needed some friendly support. He stepped closer and held her. He assured, "Your old buddy Cal is here for you, Sweetheart."

Hannah looked at Calvin and then at Sarah. She pointed, but could muster only one word, "But!"

Sarah couldn't hold back her tears. "My God, Hannah, I've found you." A tear of joy trickled down her cheek.

Happy tears flowed from Tina's eyes, too. She silently watched, and thought, *"This is so cool!"*

Calvin brushed a tear away from the corner of his eye.

Hannah began crying. She muttered, "I'm so confused. Where did you come from?"

Sarah laughed softly and said, "Duh? Wouldn't you think I came from the same place you did . . . our mother?"

Hannah was still in shock when she tried to answer. "Umm, yes . . . I think, but . . ."

Sarah raised her palm toward Hannah. "Apparently your parents did not tell you certain things, either."

Sarah put her palms together in front of her face and rested her index fingers against her chin. "Not only do you have a twin sister, but you, too, are an adopted child." She quickly added, "The same as me!"

Hannah was stunned. "You're telling me that my mom and dad are not my real mom and dad?"

Sarah explained, "Yes, we've both been adopted, and my mom and dad are not my real mom and dad, either."

Hannah could only say, "Oh my God! How can this be?"

Sarah continued, "I know this is a real shock to you, but I am sure, after a little talk, we can get everything straightened out."

Hannah pushed her fingers through her bangs. "My head is spinning."

Calvin suggested, "Why don't we find a place where we can sit and talk."

They went inside the gift shop and sat at a large table.

Hannah said, "I think I need a stiff drink."

Sarah did most of the talking. She tried her best to explain everything. Hannah was numb. She said very little in response to Sarah's explanations.

An hour later, Calvin stood up and excused himself. "I need to get back to the orchard."

Hannah stood up and gave him a good-bye hug. "It's been good to see you, Cal."

Sarah said, "Yes, It's been a pleasure to meet you, Mr. Jessup."

He waved a forgiving hand at Sarah and said, "Please, call me Calvin."

Tina said, "Good-bye, Calvin."

He waved at them, and left the gift shop.

Sarah looked at Hannah and spoke. "When I was talking to Calvin, he mentioned that your husband's name is Scott."

Hannah replied, "Yes, we've been married for over five years now."

Sarah asked, "Can I meet him?"

Hannah replied, "Scott went to Florida on a fishing trip. He won't be back until sometime next week."

Sarah said, "That's too bad. I would love to meet him. However, Tina and I have little time, so I don't see that happening during this visit. Tina must return to work on Wednesday."

Hannah said, "I am sure Scott would want to meet you. He will be as shocked as I am to find out I have a sister," She giggled, "especially a twin sister."

Sarah said, "It's too bad he is not here. I will try to come back in a week or so. I'll meet him then."

Sarah sighed, and changed the subject. "Tina and I have been on the go all day. I think I will rent a motel room in Richmond. We'll go freshen up, and then find a place to eat."

Hannah suggested, "The Richmond Motor Inn is clean and inexpensive. They have a nice lounge, too. I'm not sure if they serve food."

Tina and Sarah stood up. Sarah asked Hannah, "Could you come there later on?"

Hannah said, "Yes, I'd love to."

Sarah smiled and hugged Hannah. "We have so much to talk about."

Hannah said, "I'll see you there, umm, how about, 7:00?"

Sarah nodded. "Yes, that will be fine." She took in a deep breath and then let it out. "We will go now.

See you tonight.

Good bye."

Hannah said, "Good bye, and please drive carefully."

Tina said, "It was nice to meet you, Hannah."

Sarah and Tina left.

Hannah watched them drive away. She pushed her fingers through her bangs and said, "My God, Scott will never believe this. Umm, actually, I'm not sure I believe it either." She patted her face with her palms.

Tina drove and said, "I'd guess your head is spinning."

Sarah nodded. "Yes, and I'd bet Hannah's is, too.

Chapter Twelve
Relevancy

Hannah's cell phone rang. She could tell from the caller ID that it was Scott. She answered it, "Hello, Honey."

He asked, "Did you try to call me?"

Hannah said, "Yes. Are you sitting down? If not, you might want to find a seat. I have some news you probably won't believe."

Scott asked, "What's going on?"

She said, "I need to tell you something that might come as a shock."

He said, "Please, quit playing mind games with me. Tell me what you're talking about!"

Hannah spoke slowly and deliberately. "I found out, just today, that I have a sister, a twin sister."

There was a long silence before Scott finally said, "Sister? Did I hear you right? You never told me you had a sister! Did you say a twin sister? What's going on, Hannah?"

She said, "Honey, I honestly did not know about her. When I saw her, I was speechless.

I was working, and, out of the blue, Calvin Jessup comes walking in to the shop. He said he had a surprise for me, and asked me to step outside with him. When we got to the parking lot, he introduced me to his, little surprise; it was my sister! Her name is Sarah Lynn. My God, Honey, she looks exactly like me!"

Scott was unsure of what to say. He thought for a moment and then asked, "What did you say to her?"

Hannah said, "It shocked me. I screamed. I couldn't believe it. I didn't know what to say.

We came in the shop and sat at the table. She tried to explain everything to me. Apparently, Calvin mentioned you to her, because she asked about you. She wanted to meet you. I told her that you are fishing in Florida.

She is leaving tomorrow morning, but said she will be back to visit sometime soon. She hopes to meet you then."

Scott said, "Gee, you mean to tell me there's another beautiful angel like you in this world?"

Hannah scoffed. "Angel? Okay, Mister, what have you done? You only call me an angel when you've been a bad boy."

Scott chuckled. "I've done nothing . . . Dear. I've been a perfect angel!"

Hannah laughed and said sarcastically, "Yeah right! I know you all too well, Mr. Pillar-of-the-community. However, I will say that you are, most definitely, a perfect something or another! Now, what have you done?"

Scott quickly changed the subject. "I'll be home on Thursday. Right now, I'm on a boat in the middle of Tampa Bay."

Hannah said, "I suppose Sarah will meet you soon enough. She and her friend, Tina, invited me to come to Richmond tonight. We're having drinks at the Richmond Inn. I'll fill you in on what all is said when you get home.

Bye, Honey, I love you. And you'd better behave yourself, Mister."

Scott quipped, "Like I said, I'm a perfect angel . . . at all times. I love you, too. Bye."

Hannah looked at the clock as she hung up the phone. "Oh my, I'd better be getting home. I need a shower and a bite to eat before I go to town."

She paused and slowly shook her head. "Wow, today has absolutely blown my mind. But, it is so neat to know I have a, for real, sister."

She shook her head wildly and laughed. "Whew!"

She saw herself in a mirror behind the counter. She patted her cheeks and then boasted conceitedly. "And my, isn't Sarah a beautiful, TWIN, sister!" She crinkled her nose at herself. "And I'm such a perfect angel, too!"

She picked up the phone and called her friend Debbie.

Hannah asked, "Can you watch Brandon for a few more hours while I go to Richmond? It might be late when I pick him up."

Debbie agreed.

Hannah said, "Thanks, I'll pick him up on my way home."

Hannah whispered, "Oh my God, Debbie, I have something to tell you that you won't believe.

Today..."

Hannah went on to tell Debbie all about Sarah.

Debbie suggested that she keep Brandon overnight.

Hannah was appreciative. "That would be great. You are such a Godsend. Thank you so much.

Yes, I'll be careful.

I love you, too.

I'll tell you more tomorrow.

Bye."

She left the shop and headed home.

Hannah met Sarah in the motel lounge.

Tina ordered a round of drinks. She said to Hannah, "I love all the flowers and ornaments you have displayed outside your shop. We saw them earlier today while on our way to Richmond." She chuckled. "I almost stopped, but we were so hungry, we decided not to. I bet an unannounced visit might have proved interesting, huh?"

Hannah replied, "I'm not sure I can absorb all of this new sister and adoption stuff." She ran her fingers through her bangs. "Everything has come crashing down on me, and whew, all at once!"

She raised her eyebrows. "It's been a real head rush!"

Sarah apologized. I'm sorry. It must all seem so bizarre."

Sarah changed the subject. "Didn't you say that you're married?"

Hannah nodded. "Yes, it's been five years now, going on six."

Sarah continued, "Do you have any children?"

Hannah smiled broadly and opened her purse. "Yes, I have a son." She pulled out a picture and handed it to Sarah. Tina leaned closer to see.

Sarah smiled. "He is a handsome little fella."

Tina chimed in, "Look at those beautiful blue eyes!"

Hannah said, "His name is Brandon; Brandon Joseph. He got those big blue eyes and that coal black hair from his dad."

Tina asked, "How old is Brandon?"

Hannah replied, "He'll be four next month." She showed them another picture. "This is Scott and I when we were on our honeymoon." She chuckled. "Umm, we are both much fatter now than we were then."

She looked at Sarah. "Oh, by the way, I called Florida and talked to Scott. When I told him the news about you, he was as surprised as I was. He's definitely looking forward to meeting you."

Hannah giggled, "The little devil must have done something he shouldn't have. He called me an angel. He only ever calls me an angel when he's been a bad boy."

Sarah gave a slight smirk and replied, "Typical man."

Tina chimed in, "Yep, he's been bad or something!"

Hannah continued, "He'll be home Thursday.

He goes on this fishing trip once a year with his friends. I don't mind him going. He loves it so much. He works so hard with the landscaping business. I think he deserves a little time off every now and then. I call it his playtime."

Sarah commented, "Landscaping? All I could see at your shop was flowers and yard ornaments. Where's all the equipment?"

Hannah explained, "We own a big building in Cambridge City. That is where Scott keeps the equipment. His office is there, too. Scott and his friend, Steve, do the landscaping thing. I have nothing to do with it. I do the flowers and yard decor from my shop at the property where you were today. Our home is in Hagerstown."

Hannah, Sarah, and Tina had a wonderful evening. Time flew by as they shared stories of their past and dreams of their futures.

Hannah checked her watch. "Oh my, it's getting late. I'd better head for home. Debbie, my good friend, is watching Brandon for the night. All I have to do is go home and go to bed. Gee, it will be so quiet without Scott and Brandon being there."

Sarah looked at her watch. "Yes, by golly, it is getting late. Hey, if you want, you can stay here at the Inn with Tina and me."

Hannah declined. "No, no, I need to go home and feed the cats, but thank you for asking."

Sarah looked at Tina, who had nearly fallen asleep. "I'm glad we got a room. I hate driving at night, or in the rain for that matter." She nudged Tina. "Okay, Sleepy Head, let's go to our room."

Tina yawned and stood up. She gave another half yawn and smiled at Hannah. She stretched and said, "It's been nice to meet you, Hannah."

Hannah yawned too, and nodded. "Whew, Tina, stop that, you're making me yawn, and yes, it's been a pleasure meeting you." She looked at Sarah. "I've had such a wonderful evening. I can hardly wait until we do this again." She stood up, hugged Sarah, and handed her a business card. "Here's my phone number. Please keep in touch. I look so forward to seeing you again . . . many times."

Sarah agreed, "Yes, I've had so much fun tonight. I hope that I get to meet Scott and Brandon, um, sooner than later." Hannah left.

Sarah and Tina finished their drinks and went to their room.

The next morning, Sarah and Tina headed back to Westfield.

Tina said, "Yesterday became an overnight trip that was well worth the effort."

Sarah said with regret, "Yes. I only wish we could have found out where my mom is."

Tina gave Sarah an assuring smile. "We'll find her, and all in good time."

Sarah's cell phone rang. She quickly turned down the car radio, and answered it, "Hello?"

A male voice said, "I'm trying to reach Sarah Meeks."

Sarah replied, "This is Sarah Meeks. Who is this?"

The man said, "My name is John Rutledge. I am the son of Amanda Rutledge."

Tina saw concern in Sarah's face.

Sarah asked, "Oh my, is Amanda okay?"

John said, "She is doing fine."

Sarah sighed in relief.

John informed, "She's been resting in a nursing home for a few days. She had a touch of pneumonia. I felt that 24-hour care would be better for her."

Sarah asked, "Why are you calling me?"

John explained, "Mom gave me this number and asked me to call you. She wanted you to know that she's found some very important information about your mother. She wants you to come to Carthage."

Sarah agreed. "Of course, I'd be happy to meet with her. I'm anxious to hear what she has discovered. I'll come whenever she feels well enough to see me."

John said, "I'll be taking her home the day after tomorrow. You can visit her then."

Sarah said, "It is so good to hear that she is going home. Please, let her know that I will definitely be coming for a visit. I'll be there around noon, the day after tomorrow. Thank you so much for calling.

I'm so excited."

John said, "Very good. I'll tell her to expect you.

Oh, she asks that you please call ahead before you come."

Sarah said, "Will do, John. Thanks again. Good bye."

John said, "Good-bye," and hung up.

Tina was concerned. "I heard you mention Amanda Rutledge. Is she okay?"

Sarah said, "That was John Rutledge, Amanda's son. He says Amanda is fine, and that she has more information about my mom. I'm going to see her the day after tomorrow."

Tina frowned. "I'm sorry, but I won't be able to go with you this time. I've used up all my personal days, and I won't be able to get off work."

Sarah said, "Don't you worry, I'll be fine."

Chapter Thirteen
Resonance

Sarah woke up earlier than usual. She couldn't stop thinking about her meeting with Amanda. She tossed and turned most of the night.

She carried a fresh cup of coffee with her as she went to check the mailbox. She got the mail, and returned to the kitchen. She sat at the table and sorted through the letters. "Bills, bills, bills; gee, I'm so popular these days."

Her cell phone rang. She answered it, "Hello?"

Tina said, "Good morning."

Sarah glimpsed at the clock and giggled. "Why in the world are you calling me this early in the morning?"

Tina quipped, "I'm not up early. Umm, I haven't been to bed yet. I called so early because I remembered you are going to meet with Amanda in Carthage today. I figured you would be gone most of the day and I didn't want to forget about telling you something."

Sarah giggled again. "Duh, you dingbat, I do have a cell phone, and you could have called me any time you wanted!"

Tina said, "Oh yeah, I guess you do . . . and I could have, huh?"

Tina continued. "Anyway, I have some exciting news, and I didn't want to wait until later to tell you."

Sarah was suspicious. "What did you do?"

Tina snickered. "No, I didn't DO anything. Actually, I found something, umm, sort of."

Sarah demanded mildly, "Okay, Tina, what?"

Tina boasted, "I was at the Paramount Bar last night."

Sarah said, "And?"

Tina said with delight, "Joe, The Hunk, Bradley, and I are now an item."

Sarah slowly shook her head. "You called to tell me you got laid?"

Tina scoffed. "No, we didn't have sex . . . not yet anyway! I'm telling you, Sarah, you missed the boat on this one. Joe and I talked for hours. I am so looking forward to dating him. He is such a hunk; Grrrr!"

Sarah was happy for Tina. "Well good for you. I'd say if you take care of Mr. Hunk, and show him you are a good person, then the two of you should be great for each other. Grrrr; jeez, Tina, you sound like a silly high school girl!

Umm, look, I was about to leave. If you don't mind, I need to cut our conversation short."

Tina agreed. "No problem. Be careful driving to Carthage. Please call me when you get back. I'd like to hear what Amanda found out about your mom."

Sarah said, "When I get back, I'll probably stop by the Paramount. Drop in if you can, and we'll talk. If we don't meet up, I'll call you at home.

I do have to go, so bye, for now."

Tina echoed, "Bye."

Sarah grabbed her purse and headed out.

She had just opened her car door when her cell phone rang again. She complained, "Dang that girl!" She slammed the door shut and answered the phone. "Damn it, Tina, I have to go, I'm running late!"

A male voice spoke, "Sarah, this is Dr. Sheffield."

Sarah blurted out, "Oh my God, Dr. Sheffield! Where have you been? Why did you leave without telling me?"

He answered calmly, "I do apologize for not informing you of my transfer to Auburn University. The immediate change of employment was an unanticipated circumstance. I had to leave Westfield without giving notice to anyone. I also apologize for calling you this early."

She replied, "I'm glad you called, but, I'm heading out-of-town for the day. I'm going to…"

He interrupted, "I have important information about your Out of Body Experience."

159

Sarah said, "Oh my, please hold. I'm out by my car. I need to walk back in the house to get a pen and paper."

He agreed, "Very well."

She hurried to the house, scurried to the kitchen, found a pen and note pad, and then got back on the phone. "Whew, I'm out of breath, but go ahead, I'm listening."

Dr. Sheffield continued. "Because most catastrophic events happen close to where a person lives, I believe the accident occurred somewhere in Ohio. I have done extensive research on the road sign you mentioned. However, the letters and their combination are not so unique. Actually, there are hundreds of possibilities. Further, you said the sign looked as though someone had shot it with bullets. If that were true, I would say the sign must have been in a rural setting, or at least on a road that is not a very busy one. You also said that you thought the road was gravel or stone. This sounds like a rural road and not an interstate highway.

There's one more thing. You mentioned nothing about snow or freezing cold temperatures. Therefore, I believe we can drop winter as a possible time for the accident. I know this is not much, but, it is a small step forward."

To Sarah, the new information was disappointing. She said, "We are no closer to knowing anything of value than we were before you left."

He contended, "This information is more significant than you may believe. We simply need to go ahead with our investigation. Continuing is the only way we can find the answers."

She said, "I must tell you something." She took a deep breath, and then let it out. "I have, and for some time now, been considering what you said about this Out of Body thing driving me crazy. After you abandoned me, I lost all hope."

Dr. Sheffield quickly defended himself. "I didn't abandon you."

Sarah ignored his comment and continued. "Right now, I have other things going on in my life. Therefore, I've decided not to worry so much about the Out of Body Experience. I need to move on with my life. Besides, you said I couldn't change my fate, right?"

He pleaded, "No, you mustn't stop! We must continue searching for the truth. Isn't finding out the time and place of your impending death important enough to command your attention? Isn't it of the utmost interest to learn and understand every detail, so we might prevent the accident?

Dear God, Sarah, we MUST try to divert the time and manner of your death!

I am sorry you believe that I abandoned you, but I truly did have to leave without much notice.

Although I am no longer in Ohio, I assure you, I am continuing my research. I still need your help. Please, we must continue!"

Sarah smirked. "You only care about your book!

You took away my ability to have Out of Body Experiences, and in doing so, you broke the faith I had in you. You destroyed my trust.

Besides, I'm not so sure I want to know when or where I will die. Didn't you say that death is the fate of all humanity? Doesn't dying make my destiny irrelevant?"

Sarah ran her fingers through her hair, shut her eyes, and stated, "I'm not pursuing this anymore." She glimpsed at her watch. "I'm sorry, Dr. Sheffield, but I'm leaving town. I'm running very late for my appointment. I do need to go. Thank you for calling. I wish you well in your new job at Auburn."

Dr. Sheffield became angry. He demanded, "NO! You must not stop!"

Sarah said calmly, "Good-bye,   Dr. Sheffield."

She heard him scream out as she pulled the phone away from her ear. "NO!"

She shrugged her shoulders and hung up.

Sarah arrived in Carthage.

Amanda greeted her with a prompt scolding. "I thought I asked you to call me before you left Westfield?"

Surprised by Amanda's comment, Sarah apologized. "I'm sorry. I was running late. I felt that a phone call would delay my arrival even more. If my being late is an inconvenience, I can leave."

Amanda grimaced, waved her hand at Sarah, and said woefully, "For heaven's sake, listen to my silly attitude. I'm getting so grouchy in my old age." She reached out and patted Sarah on the shoulder. "My goodness, you are here, and that is the important thing.

Bless your heart."

Amanda motioned. "Come in, Sweetheart, you're letting the flies in!"

Amanda took three steps, abruptly stopped, and whirled.

Sarah didn't anticipate Amanda's actions. She nearly ran into her. "Oops!"

Amanda held her hands high in the air and exclaimed, "Give me five, Miss Sarah Lynn!"

Reluctantly, Sarah gave Amanda a gentle high-five. She was unsure of Amanda's actions. She thought, "Why is Amanda acting so differently than she has at other times."

Amanda dropped her hands and placed them on her hips. "I have some good news for you." She whirled again, and went to the kitchen.

Sarah eased her way in to the dining room.

Amanda returned with a cake in hand. She sat the cake on the dining room table. "I wanted to know when you were coming, so I could have the candles burning for our celebration."

Sarah consoled, "Aww, I'm so sorry. I didn't mean to spoil your surprise." It then dawned on Sarah what Amanda had just said. She asked curiously, "Celebration? What celebration might that be?"

Amanda dressed up the cake with a few candles and began lighting them. With the candles burning, Amanda gave Sarah a broad grin. She reached out to hug her, and announced, "I have found your mother!"

Sarah was elated and said happily, "You have?" She patted her hands with excitement, and then gave Amanda a loving hug. "This is such wonderful news."

Sarah released her grasp and asked, "Where is she?"

Amanda held up a finger and answered, "She is alive and well, and living in Indiana. She lives in a town called Beech Grove. She works as a nurse in Community Hospital, which is in Greensburg, Indiana.

Bless her heart."

Amanda boasted, "You may hug me and kiss me in a second, but first you had better blow out these candles before they ruin my delicious icing."

Sarah bent down and blew out the candles.

Amanda clapped again, and then scooted a chair away from the table. "Please sit here while I cut the cake."

Sarah sat down. "You have been working very hard to help me. How can I ever repay you?"

Amanda put her hand on Sarah's shoulder. "Wait, Sweetheart, I have more to tell you." She reached in to a bag that was beneath the table. She pulled out a large tan-colored wide-brimmed hat. There was a long bluish-gray ostrich feather flowing from the band of the hat.

Sarah smiled when she saw the feather.

Amanda put the hat on her head and gently stroked her hand down the length of the feather. She crinkled her nose at Sarah and said, "Not only do I deserve a feather in my cap, I also deserve the biggest feather I could find." She stroked the feather again. "Do you like it?"

Amanda's actions were out of character. Sarah had assumed Amanda to be a more refined and reserved woman.

Sarah folded her fingers together and replied in a very distinguished voice. "It is very becoming, Mrs. Rutledge!"

Amanda sat in a chair next to Sarah. "I have even more wonderful news."

Sarah replied, "You do?"

Amanda nodded and explained, "I confided in my son, John, about your situation. He is the one who thought that your mother might be in the medical field." She waved her hand in the air and said with amazement, "Where he ever got that notion, I'll never know." She lowered her hand and continued. "Anyway, he spent quite a bit of time searching the Internet.

Bless his heart.

He found your mother's name on a list of graduates who attended a nursing school in Indianapolis."

Amanda hugged Sarah. She released her hug and held Sarah's hands. "During his search, John found your mother's last known address." She smiled and looked in Sarah's eyes. "It would be my guess that your mother is living there this very minute."

Sarah gave Amanda's hands a gentle squeeze. Her eyes welled up with tears of joy. She replied, "Oh my! This is such happy news!" A tear trickled down her smiling face.

Amanda wiped the tear away. "Bless your heart."

Sarah hugged Amanda. "I'm not sure what to say. I suppose, at the very least, I should say thank you. And, I mean that from the bottom of my heart."

Amanda threw her arms up and roared, "Woo hoo, I'm as proud as a peacock!" She snickered, stroked the feather again, waggled her head, and asked, "Or, should I say, Ostrich?"

Sarah couldn't help but giggle. "My Goodness, Amanda, you're feeling very good today."

Sarah heard a knock on the front door. She turned to see a man come in the house.

The man said, "Mom, it's me, John."

John noticed Sarah, and apologized. "Oh, please forgive me. Am I interrupting something?" Sarah replied, "Not at all." She stood up and reached out to shake hands. "We have not officially met, but we have talked on the phone. I am Sarah Meeks, and you, I presume, are John Rutledge."

John smiled. "Yes, I am John Rutledge." He asked, "Did Mom give you the good news?"

Amanda interrupted, "Whoopty-do, good for you! Sarah Lynn is gonna win!

Bless her heart!"

Sarah smiled politely and said, "Your mom is in very good spirits today."

John was embarrassed. He sighed, "Oh dear!" He looked at his mom and then at Sarah. "I assure you, my mother does not drink in excess. Her doctor changed her medication a few days ago. He advised me of this sudden mood swing." John gave a wry smile. "I can see I need to have her dosage adjusted.

Bless her heart."

Sarah giggled. "She has, indeed, been acting slightly out of character this afternoon." She looked John in the eyes. "But I mean that in a good way."

John nodded. "Yes."

He saw a piece of paper with the name Marsha Langley and an address written on it. He picked it up and handed it to Sarah. "Here, this is for you. I am sorry, but I was unable to find your mother's phone number."

Sarah was grateful, and shook hands with John. "You have been such a great help. How may I repay you for your kind effort?"

John raised his hands slightly, shook his head, and said, "You owe me nothing. I am glad that I could be of help. However, may I ask that once you have met with your mother, that you give Mom an update on what's going on? I am sure she would appreciate a follow-up visit."

Sarah agreed. "I have every intention of letting Amanda know what happens. I also intend to have pictures taken. I will share those as well. Hopefully my Mom and my sister, Hannah, and I can get together very soon."

Sarah saw Amanda twirl around and plop down on a chair. Sarah put her hand over her mouth and snickered, "Oh my!"

John shook his head and chuckled. "Umm, I better get her to lie down for a little while. Then, I'd better call and have her prescription changed."

Sarah smiled proudly. "Aww, bless her heart."

Sarah smiled at John and consoled, "It appears that taking care of your mom will be a handful. Do you need my help?"

John shook his head. "I can handle her. Thanks for the offer."

Sarah said, "Okay then." She turned toward the door. "I do need to go. It's been a pleasure meeting you."

Before Sarah left, she walked over to Amanda and gave her a hug. "I am going now. I will keep in touch."

Amanda waggled her head. "Bless your heart."

Sarah returned to Westfield. She stopped at the Paramount Bar where she found a table and ordered a rum and coke. She decided to call Hannah and tell her the good news about finding their mother.

Hannah answered the phone. "Hi, I was just now thinking about you."

Sarah admitted, "Hmmm, I was thinking of you too. There must be some sort of a connection; do you think?"

Hannah laughed and answered, "Whatever."

Sarah said, "I have some great news."

Hannah said, "Hang on a second." She turned down the volume of her stereo. "Okay, now I can hear you better."

Sarah repeated, "I have some great news. I found out where our mom lives."

The news thrilled Hannah. "That's great. Where is she?"

Sarah said, "Our mom is a nurse, and she works in a hospital in Greensburg, Indiana. She is now living in Beech Grove, Indiana."

Hannah said, "Beech Grove? That's only 40-some miles from here. Gee, when I go to Terre Haute, or sometimes Crawfordsville, I drive right through there. It's a very small town."

Sarah said, "I have her address. I'd like to go visit her."

Hannah kept silent for a short time.

Sarah broke the quiet. "Hello? Are you there?"

Hannah answered, "Yes, I'm here. I'm sorry; I was thinking about what might happen when we meet our mom for the first time. You know, Sarah, Mom may not want to meet us. We may bring up a past for her that she has long since tried to forget."

Sarah agreed, "Oh my, you are so right." She added, "If we go barging in to her life, and she's married, we might unintentionally cause her many problems. What do you think we should do?"

Hannah said, "I was thinking; maybe we should send her a discrete letter."

Sarah agreed. "Yes, a letter might be the best way to begin. It would forewarn her."

Hannah added, "A private meeting with us might save Mom from a bad or embarrassing situation. We need to meet her on her own terms."

Sarah said, "Yes, we should give her a chance to prepare the people she has in her personal life. Do you think she's married?"

Hannah assumed, "I'd say there's a good possibility. She might even have children, too." Sarah realized and mentioned, "We could have sisters . . . or even a brother."

Hannah said, "Yes."

Sarah asked, "Would you write the letter?"

Hannah spoke confidently. "I will, if you're not comfortable with writing one."

Sarah admitted, "I would, but I'm not sure of what words to say that would best explain the situation."

Hannah accepted the responsibility. "Okay, I'll write the letter. I'll call when I'm done and read it to you. If you want to add something, I'll be happy to change it."

Sarah liked the idea. "That will be perfect.

If you have a pen, I will give you Mom's address."

Hannah said, "I will write the letter tomorrow, and then call you tomorrow night. What time is best for you?"

Sarah replied, "Any time after 6:00 will be good."

Hannah said, "Okay. I will talk to you tomorrow night."

Hannah wrote down the address.

The girls hung up.

Hannah began formulating the letter in her mind.

Sarah sat quietly and sipped her drink. She thought about her mom.

Tina and Joe showed up. Sarah invited them to sit with her.

Tina said, "So, tell me what Amanda had to say."

Sarah updated Tina. She mentioned the letter that Hannah will be writing. She gave a concerned smile and said, "I hope Mom will want to meet us." She frowned slightly and admitted, "Our mom may not want anything to do with us. She may not have said anything to her husband about the adoptions, that is, if she's even married."

Tina gave her support. "I am sure your mom will want to meet you, no matter what the circumstances are.

Wouldn't it be cool if you do have brothers or sisters?"

Sarah took a deep breath. She slowly let it out. "Time will tell."

Chapter Fourteen
The Reunion

Hannah wrote a lengthy letter to her mom. As promised, she called and read it for Sarah to scrutinize.

Sarah suggested, "We should add our phone numbers and addresses; that way, if Mom wants to call or write, she'll have what she needs to do so."

Hannah made the change and said, "I'll mail the letter first thing in the morning."

They could only hope and pray that their mom would respond.

[A week later]

Hannah frantically dialed the phone.

She listened. The phone rang three times. She complained, "Come on Sarah, answer the phone!"

Sarah answered, "Hello, Hannah. How are you today..."

Hannah blurted out, "I got a letter from Mom!

She can't wait to meet us!

She still lives in Beech Grove!

She's a Registered Nurse!

She's..."

Sarah giggled and interrupted. "Slow down, Hannah, we have plenty of time to talk."

Short of breath, Hannah exclaimed, "Whew, I'm sorry, but, I'm so excited. I'll read the letter.

Dear Hannah and Sarah,

I am so happy to know that my babies are now young women. I hope that, soon, we can get together for a long talk.

Years ago, some very difficult circumstances developed in my life. There were irrational decisions made, and regrettable actions taken, which influenced all of our lives. Those decisions and actions were beyond your control. I must say though, not many days passed without my thinking of those darkest days.

Instead of my trying to explain them in this letter, I feel it would be better if we discuss those situations in a friendly and personal atmosphere.

I invite both of you to come to my home. If you do not wish to do so, I could come to Hagerstown. I will let you girls decide. Whatever works best for you will be fine by me.

I am sure there are many questions that need answered. However, patience is a virtue, and for me, waiting until we can all be together will be the best way to avoid misunderstood statements.

However, I will not be so cruel as to say nothing at all about me.

Several years ago I got married, but I am now divorced. I am in good health, both physically and mentally. Any other information about me is less important, and can wait until later.

Might I suggest that we meet over the Thanksgiving holiday?

I will include my phone number below. Please call me and let me know what you girls plan. The best time to call is after 8:00 in the evening. You will have a better chance of reaching me during the week. I work overtime as much as I possibly can, so, you will likely not reach me on the weekends.

After all these years, I look forward to being with my daughters. I cried so many times, believing that I would never see either of you again.

God has surely chosen to bless us all!

I love you with all my heart and soul.

See you soon,

Marsha Langley,
Your mom"

Hannah squealed, "Isn't this exciting?"

A relieved Sarah said, "This is so great. I can come to Indiana at any time. Thanksgiving would be good, but I'll leave that decision up to you."

Hannah agreed, "I will call Mom and ask her to come to my house on Thanksgiving Day."

Sarah asked, "Will you call and let me know when you have confirmed the plans?"

Hannah said, "Yes, no problem.

If you have a pen, I'll give you Mom's phone number." She added, "If it wasn't for you, we may have never known about each other . . . or Mom."

Sarah replied, "Fate seems to have a way of getting things done."

Hannah said, "Fate? Whatever!

I will call Mom around 9:00."

Sarah said, "Very good.

Bye, for now, I love you."

Hannah said, "Bye, I love you, too."

Scott walked up to Hannah and kissed her.

"So, the big reunion will be at Thanksgiving?"

Hannah smiled, "Yes, Thanksgiving Day."

[Thanksgiving weekend]

Sarah called Hannah on Wednesday night before Thanksgiving. She asked, "Would you like for me to come over tomorrow and help you with the dinner preparation?"

Hannah said, "Sure, come on over, but there's no need to come terribly early because I'll be cooking all morning. I won't put the turkey in the oven until around nine. Mom will be here about noon. She has to work tonight, and wants to get some sleep before she comes."

Sarah said, "We have a very good bakery here. I thought I might pick up a nice apple or peach pie."

Hannah agreed. "That will be perfect. Mom is bringing the rolls and the noodles. I'll make the dressing. You and I can do the potatoes and the green bean casserole."

Sarah said, "Don't forget the baked beans, and the deviled eggs."

Hannah grumbled, "Crap, I forgot about the eggs. Can you pick up a dozen for me?"

[Thanksgiving morning]

Sarah approached Hannah's house with a sack under her arm and a pie in each hand. Hannah held the door open for her. Brandon was holding on to his mom's pant leg. Sarah smiled at the shy Brandon as she walked inside. Brandon curiously eyed Sarah. He hugged his mom's leg and looked back and forth between her and Sarah; it was strange to see another person who looked exactly like his mom.

Hannah put her hand on Brandon's head.

"This is Brandon." She looked at him and said, "Brandon, this is your aunt Sarah."

Sarah smiled at Brandon again. She kept her eyes on him as she handed the pies to Hannah. "Hi, Brandon; it's nice to meet you."

She looked at Hannah. "I didn't know which pie would be better, so I brought one of each, an apple, and a peach." She pulled the bag from beneath her arm. "I hope you wanted large eggs." She set the eggs on a chair. She took a small sack from her purse and handed it to Brandon. "Here, this is for you."

Brandon looked at his mom, as if to ask permission to take the gift.

Hannah nodded. "Yes, you can have it."

Brandon opened the sack. His face lit up when he saw a toy truck inside. He smiled, tore open the sack, held up the truck, and made noises like the revs of an engine. He stepped on the bag when he raced away to play.

Sarah picked up the crumpled sack. She picked up the bag with the eggs. "He is so cute!"

Hannah nodded, "He sure is!" She headed to the kitchen with the pies.

Sarah asked, "Can I meet your husband?" She followed Hannah.

Hannah set the pies on the counter and apologized. "I'm so sorry, but Scott is not here. He went hunting with his friends. He goes every Thanksgiving morning. He should be back in time to eat."

Sarah gave an understanding nod. "So, what can I do to help with the meal?"

The two sisters tried to keep a conversation, but the anticipation of meeting their mom for the first time had both of them watching the clock. Hannah made a third trip to look out the front room window. She returned, shook her head, and groaned. "Not yet."

With a worried tone, Sarah said, "I hope she isn't running late or having trouble or something.

This sitting and waiting is driving me crazy.

Have you checked the turkey?"

Hannah looked at the clock and snickered. "Yes, I've checked it three times in the last twenty minutes!"

Brandon ran up to his mom and twirled a toy plane in her face.

She pushed the plane away. "Stop it, Brandon; go play in your room!"

Brandon flew the plane in front of Sarah, made a jet sound, and sped away.

Sarah ran her fingers through her bangs.

She wondered, *"Will Mom even like us?"*

Time crept by . . . oh so slowly.

Two hours later, Sarah heard a car. "I think Mom is here."

They rushed out on the porch to greet their mom. Brandon followed. He peeked out from behind his mom's leg.

In unison, Sarah and Hannah stepped off the porch and walked toward their mom's car.

Brandon kept close.

Marsha got out of her car and stared at the girls. She wiped away a tear. "I have found my babies!" She stepped toward them with her arms open wide. The girls hurried to her and hugged her. There was not a dry eye among them.

Marsha released her hug and held hands with her daughters. She looked at them with a broad smile. "I thought I would never see you girls again."

Hannah tugged her mom's arm. "Come in the house."

Marsha paused and said, "Wait, I brought some food." She turned away, went to the car, and then returned.

Sarah reached out for the dish her mom was carrying. "Let me take that for you." She smiled and noticed; "I love your sweater. And, your hair looks so nice. Did you make these noodles?"

Hannah took the bag of rolls. "Let's go to the kitchen."

Marsha gave a little laugh. "I slaved all the way to the grocery store to get those homemade egg noodles."

Hannah giggled.

In the living room, Hannah picked up Brandon and said to him, "This is your Grandma Marsha. Isn't she beautiful?"

Brandon squirmed, so Hannah set him down.

Marsha said, "You are quite a handsome little man. I will be proud to call you my grandson."

Brandon stretched his arms out like the wings of a plane, made a noise like a jet, and soared away.

Marsha and Sarah followed Hannah to the kitchen.

Marsha stood before her daughters and smiled proudly. "Look at you girls. You are both so beautiful."

Sarah said, "You are, too, Mom."

Hannah said, "Scott will be here in a little while."

Marsha waved her hand toward Hannah and said, "Let me guess, he's hunting, right?"

Hannah nodded, "Yep, the traditional Thanksgiving excuse. I think men plan to go hunting so they won't have to help with the cooking."

An hour later, Scott walked in the back door.

Brandon ran and jumped up in his daddy's arms. Scott gave Brandon a quick hug and set him back on the floor. "Now, go to your room and play." Brandon sped away.

Hannah grabbed Scott's arm and introduced him. She pointed at each of them as she said,

"Mom, and Sarah, this is Scott. Scott this is my mom, Marsha, and my sister, Sarah."

Scott shook hands with them. "I need to get out of these hunting clothes. I'll be back in a minute." He left the room.

Marsha said to Hannah, "My, he is a very good -looking man."

Sarah chimed in by asking, "You said that you've been together for eleven years?"

Hannah opened the oven door to check on the turkey. "Yes, eleven years, and we've been married six."

Scott returned. He had overheard the last part of the conversation. He said sarcastically, "If marriage is an institution, then, I've been institutionalized for six long years!"

Marsha and Sarah laughed at Scott's comment.

Hannah swatted his arm and replied, "Aww, you poor baby, it's been such a miserable life, hasn't it?"

Scott grinned. He paused in thought, and then joked, "I'm a prisoner of love." He gave Hannah a quick kiss on the cheek. He created an exaggerated sad look on his face, and added, "Poor me; Right?"

He looked at Marsha and Sarah as he moved toward the doorway. "Umm, before I get into more trouble than I already am, I'd better try to make a break for it. Maybe I can escape the wrath of

Hannah. You'll find me shackled to my recliner, slaving away with the TV remote."

Hannah grumbled, "You'd better make your getaway while you still can, Mister!" She threw a dishtowel at him, pointed toward the living room, and scolded, "Go watch TV . . . and behave!"

Scott popped his head back in the kitchen to say, "Missed me!" He then fled to the living room. Marsha and Sarah snickered at Scott and Hannah's friendly little spat.

Idle chatter among the women consumed the time until after dinner.

After eating, Brandon kept his distance and played with his toys on the floor.

When the meal was over, they cleaned the dishes and put them away.

Sarah praised, "Gee, at least Scott knows how to help with the dishes."

Marsha said, "You have trained him very well, Hannah. I am proud of you."

Scott mumbled, "Yeah, right."

They all gathered in the living room.

Scott brought a chair from the kitchen and sat next to Hannah, who was sitting at the end of the couch.

Brandon sat on his mother's lap.

Marsha said, "That was a very nice dinner."

When Sarah sat down, she let out a muttered scream, "Oh," and jumped back up quickly. She reached down and picked up a toy metal plane.

Scott chuckled, and Hannah giggled, "Oops!"

Sarah handed the plane to Brandon.

"Umm, is this yours?"

Brandon smiled and accepted the plane.

Sarah double-checked the chair for other foreign objects before sitting down again.

Scott praised, "The turkey was excellent, Honey."

Hannah replied, "Thank you."

Silence lingered.

Sarah looked at her mom, put her palms together, and said, "I guess I need to tell how I found you and Hannah."

Marsha nodded as she smiled. She said nothing.

Sarah began her story from the day of the tornados in Westfield. She mentioned Tina and Amanda Rutledge. She continued her story up to the day she met Hannah for the first time.

Hannah took the story from there, and continued it to the time of the letter she had written to her mom.

Marsha listened patiently. She did not interrupt either of the girls.

Hannah looked at Sarah. "I have some questions, but Mom deserves a chance to talk."

Sarah agreed. "Yes, and maybe along the way we can find some answers to a few of our questions."

Marsha stood up. "I will be right back. I have to get something from my car."

Hannah asked, "Can I get anyone something to drink?"

Sarah said, "Tea for me please."

Marsha said, "Tea is fine for me. I'll have mine without sugar, please."

Marsha left the house.

Sarah stood up, stretched her arms and back, and yawned.

Scott said, "I think I could use a nap." He leaned back in his chair and closed his eyes.

Hannah went to get the drinks.

Marsha returned with a shoebox in her hands. She sat on the couch and set the box beside her. Hannah delivered the drinks and sat in a chair.

Sarah sat at the end of the couch.

Hannah poked Scott in the ribs. "Wake up Mister."

Scott sat up.

Brandon went to his bedroom to play.

Marsha took a deep breath, and then let it out. "Okay, I'll start at the point where I met your father." She folded her fingers together, and began.

"When I was fifteen years old, I was attending New Castle High School. Your father, Marcus Joseph Bangston, was a junior, attending Anderson North High School. We met at a pregame rally for a football game. New Castle was playing host to Anderson North. Mark approached me first. I thought he was the most handsome person I'd ever seen."

Marsha opened the box. She handed a picture to Sarah. Hannah leaned over to see.

Marsha explained, "Your father and I began seeing each other a few weeks before that picture was taken. Mark was so gentle and kind. I fell deeply in love with him. We were inseparable. It was as though someone had tied our hearts together, and they were beating as one."

Sarah exclaimed, "Aww that is so sweet!"

Marsha continued. "All of our friends believed that one day he and I would be married." She raised her index finger. "But, I wound up pregnant." She frowned. "Mark and I tried to hide it. I even quit school so nobody could see I was having a baby.

Mark's family was very influential and would have no part of him being involved with me." She said sarcastically, "They had bigger and better plans for their precious son!" She shook her head slightly, and continued, "If they were to ever find out that Mark was the father of my baby, there would have been some major issues.

Mark received a scholarship to play football at Indiana University. I was so afraid that if his family ever found out about the baby, he would lose his chance for college. I was getting big as a barn, and could no longer hide the fact that I was pregnant. That's when I decided to run away to Ohio. I found out, a few weeks later, that I was having twins. I was so scared. I had no insurance, no education, no job, and I believed that once Mark entered college, he would forget all about me.

One of the nurses at Cincinnati Mercy Hospital introduced me to Amanda Rutledge. Amanda counseled me throughout the remaining weeks of my pregnancy. She was a good and wholesome person.

Bless her heart!

After you girls were born, I faced a very real and uncertain future."

Marsha handed a paper to Sarah and another to Hannah. "Those are your birth certificates."

Hannah read hers and handed it to Sarah. "Um, this one is yours, and you must have mine."

Sarah switched.

Marsha continued, "I assure you, the decision to give up my babies was the most difficult thing I have ever done. Nonetheless, I had to do what I felt was best for you girls. I was so desperate. Giving up my babies took my very soul. Amanda promised to find good homes and good parents for each of you. I trusted her and believed her. Only the two of you can say whether she did well or not.

I cried for weeks."

Sarah hugged her mom.

Marsha admitted, "My mom and dad let me move back in with them, but I had no ambition. I felt so empty.

When Mark found out that I gave you girls up for adoption, he was livid. He began drinking heavily. He didn't seem to care much about life. He totally abandoned our relationship.

A year later, he went on a drinking binge. He had a wreck. He was speeding on his motorcycle in the park. He hit a tree. The crash killed him instantly. That was a very sad day in my life."

Marsha pulled a stack of papers from the box. "These are the newspaper articles about your dad. You'll find his high school graduation notices in there. You will also find the story about his wreck; and of course, the obituary is in there, too.

One of you will have to make copies for the other."

Marsha put her hands on her cheeks. She took a deep breath and then let it out. She continued. "My mom's church gave me the opportunity to take night classes. I hoped to become a nurse. They paid for my tuition at the IUPUI School of Nursing in Indianapolis. I went to classes four nights each week. I eventually got my license as an LP. I worked and saved my money so I could complete my training to become a registered nurse. I achieved that goal, and I am now an RN.

Somewhere along the way, I finally got over Mark's death. I met a handsome young man named Shaun Wilkes. We got married, but it never worked out. We divorced, and I moved to Beech Grove.

I got a job working as a nurse at Greensburg Community Hospital." She quickly raised her hands in the air. "And here I am."

Marsha pulled two more envelopes from the box. "These are the original adoption consent forms."

Sarah reached out and took the letters.

Marsha said, "I will let you girls look at them, but, I want to keep the originals for myself.

I can mail copies to you if you want them.

Everything else, you can keep."

Hannah moved to sit beside her mom. "You have answered many of my questions. I still have a few others, but they can wait for another day. Right now, I'd rather spend the rest of the day enjoying your company.

Would you care for a piece of pie?"

Marsha said, "Yes, a nice piece of pie would hit the spot."

Marsha kept her head still, and gazed back and forth between Hannah and Sarah. "I know you girls were probably counting on me to stay longer, but I've been asked to work the weekend. I couldn't turn it down. I'll be paid triple time for working on the holiday weekend." She looked at her watch. I will be heading back to Beech Grove in maybe an hour or so."

Hannah and Sarah moaned in unison. "OH!"

Marsha said, "I'm so sorry, but I need the money."

Scott popped his head up and said, "Did I hear someone mention pie?"

Hannah got up and said, "I'm heading to the kitchen." She looked at Scott. "I'll bring you a piece; do you want apple or peach?"

Scott said, umm, I'd take some of the apple pie, please." He quipped, "The only peaches I prefer are the ones who wear bikinis, and live in Georgia!"

Hannah nodded. "I am sure you do, Mr. Stud Muffin!"

Marsha snickered and repeated Hannah's comment, "Stud muffin; Oh my word!"

Brandon raced through the living room and in to the kitchen.

Sarah began reading the newspaper articles. "I ate too much for lunch. I think I'll pass on the pie."

A short time later, Sarah called to let Tina know how the reunion had gone.

All-too-soon, the time came for Marsha to leave.

Tears flowed once again, but all agreed that the day had been a blessing.

Brandon watched out the window as his new grandma drove away. He waved and said softly, "Bye!"

Hannah sat down with Scott to watch a movie. Sarah joined them.

Soon after the movie ended, Sarah left. She returned to Westfield, wondering when she would see her mom again.

Chapter Fifteen
As Fate Would Have It

Although Sarah had found her real mom and her sister, she could not ignore the undying love she felt for her adoptive mother. On many occasions, she would visit the park, trying to fill the void left by her mom's death. She would talk aloud, believing and hoping that, in some way, her mom would hear her heartfelt words. Much to her dismay, none of those memorable visits could appease her in the way that an Out of Body Experience could.

She blamed Dr. Sheffield for denying her access to her mom. It was he, who placed the psychic suggestion on her mind, which blocks her ability to have Out of Body Experiences.

She despised him.

[At the park]

Sarah sat on her favorite park bench and watched the children play. Her little squirrel friend came scurrying down a tree to greet her. She saw the squirrel and smiled. She pulled a small bag of treats from her pocket. She tossed the unshelled peanuts, one at a time, on the ground. The squirrel watched, and began retrieving the tasty snacks. He would eat the savory nut, and then drop the empty shell. He'd bristle his tail, and scamper across the grass in search of another one. She thought, "I wish Mom were here to see you, Little Friend."

Thoughts of Dr. Sheffield entered her mind. Almost instantly, she went from being happy to being angry. She pounded her fist on the bench, and spoke her mind aloud. "Damn you Dr. Sheffield! It is you who keeps me from being with my mom." She threw the remaining peanuts on the ground and crumpled the empty bag in her hands. She tossed the bag in the trash as she walked away. The squirrel scurried up the side of a tree and watched her leave the park.

At her car, she pulled her cell phone from her pocket and turned it on. She noticed there were several missed calls. She read the list and muttered, "Hannah, Hannah, Tina, Hannah, unknown, Tina, Hannah, Hannah Tina, Tina. Jeez, I'm glad I turned my phone off. No wonder it was so peaceful in the park."

She sat in her car, but did not start the engine. Rather, she decided to call and find out what is so important to have Tina and Hannah call so often.

She called Tina first.

Tina answered. "Where have you been, Girl? Your phone has been off all day!"

Sarah said, "I shut the phone off when I got to the park. What did you want?"

Tina asked, "Are you still going to Indiana next week?"

Sarah answered, "Yes, I'm going to see Hannah and my mom for a few days. I'll be staying at the Richmond Inn.

Why?"

Tina asked, "Can Joe and I follow you? I want Joe to meet Hannah and your mother. In fact, neither of us has met your mom. We'd love to spend a couple of days with you, that is, if you don't mind?"

Sarah replied, "You silly girl, you know I wouldn't mind."

Tina continued, "Good. I thought so. I was hoping that you were going to stay at the Richmond Motor Inn because I'd book a room for Joe and me. After we've spent some time with you and your family, Joe and I will head south to Myrtle Beach."

Tina had a quick thought. "Hey, you can come with us to Myrtle Beach if you'd like? We'd love your company."

Sarah laughed. "Slow down, Tina, my mind can only comprehend so much information at one time."

Tina apologized. "Sorry."

Sarah said, "Yes, I am staying at the Motor Inn, but, I am leaving for Indiana earlier than I had planned. Traffic is better in the morning, especially on a Friday. So, I will be leaving in the morning and not the afternoon. If that were okay with you, then yes, I would love for you and Joe to go with me.

195

And, yes, I am certain that Hannah will like Joe.

And, yes, I am sure Mom would like to meet you and Joe. She would definitely enjoy meeting anyone I consider a friend.

And, finally, NO, I do not have the money to go to Myrtle Beach, but thank you for asking.

Whew, did I miss anything?"

Tina said, "Okay, Friday morning it will be. Joe and I will meet you at your house. We will follow you to Richmond. We could eat lunch somewhere along the way."

Sarah said, "That will be great. I am leaving at 7:00 am. We could stop at Sam's Barbecue Pit, like we did the last time."

Tina agreed. "Oh yes, I remember Sam's; the pulled pork was excellent. Joe loves barbecue, too. The plan is set. We'll be at your house early Friday morning. I will call the Inn tonight and reserve our room. I bet we'll have some good times with Hannah and your mom."

Sarah said, "Um, party with Hannah, yes, but with Mom, I doubt it. I'm sure Mom would enjoy being with us, but she's not much of a late-night partier."

Tina said, "We shall see. Your mom may surprise you. Anyway, we'll be at your house Friday.

Bye, for now."

Sarah said, "Good-bye," and hung up.

Sarah called Hannah.

Hannah answered, "I've been trying to get in touch with you all day. Are you okay?"

Sarah said, "Boy, I turn my phone off for one day and, suddenly, all the world needs to call and talk to me."

Hannah said, "Huh? What are you talking about?"

Before Sarah could answer, Hannah continued. "Are you still coming here on Friday? The reason I ask is that Scott will be gone for the weekend. We could go out partying on Friday night."

Sarah laughed and teased, "When the cat's away, the mice will play."

Hannah replied, "Whatever. But hey, it's my turn for a little playtime."

Sarah mentioned, "By the way, Tina and her boyfriend, Joe, are coming with me. They will be staying at the Motor Inn, too. They want to stay a couple of days, and then head south to Myrtle Beach. Tina wants you to meet Joe, and neither of them has met our mom."

Hannah giggled, Maybe we could talk Joe into staying in the hotel while us girls have a night out."

Sarah said, "Don't count on it. These days Tina and Joe are inseparable. She is convinced that Joe is some love God or something. She says he is awesome in bed."

Hannah kidded. "Oh my, if Joe is so good, then maybe we should let him party with us!" She snickered. "Listen to me. I can't believe I said that! Please, don't tell Tina."

Sarah ignored Hannah's comment and said, "It'll be fun. I'm hoping to have a good time with my sister and my mom and my friends."

Hannah said, "Very good. I'll be looking for you on Friday."

Tina and Joe met Sarah on Friday as planned. Lunch was excellent at Sam's Barbecue Pit.

Tina and Sarah's rooms at the Inn were on separate floors. Poor Joe had to manage three flights of stairs for each trip he made from their car to the room. First, he carried the luggage. Next were the lap top computers. Then, there were two trips for the coolers.

Sarah was able to park directly in front of her first level room. She called to let Hannah know they had arrived.

Hannah answered the phone, but before she could say a word, Sarah announced, "We're here, and we'll be at your house around five."

Hannah said, "Scott left this morning. He'll be gone until sometime Sunday, um, I'm guessing, probably late evening.

I am so ready to get out on the town." She admitted, "It will be so nice to not have to listen to Scott snoring all night.

Well, I'd better let you go. Maybe you'd like to relax and have a drink or something with Joe and Tina."

Sarah asked, "Have you called Mom yet?"

Hannah answered, "Mom will be here tomorrow around noon." Hannah laughed. "Mom told me that this will be one of the few times in the past 20 years that she's taken a weekend off from working overtime. Anyway, I'm glad you made it here safely. Tell Tina, I am glad she and Joe came. I am looking forward to seeing her, and meeting Joe. What is it she calls him? Is it, The Hunk? Jeez!

Bye for now."

Sarah said, "Yep, he's The Hunk, and I will tell her. We'll see you in a while. I love you.

Good-bye."

Hannah said, "I love you, too.

Bye."

Sarah led the way for Joe and Tina. They arrived at Hannah's house at 5:20.

Tina introduced Joe. "Hannah this is Joe Bradley. Joe, this is Hannah Perkins."

Joe smiled and said, "Howdy."

Hannah gave a little smile and said, "Hi, Joe.

Wow, Tina, you sure do know where to find the good-looking ones."

Tina boasted, "He's a real hunk, isn't he?"

Joe shook his head, pulled Tina close with his right arm, and hugged her around the waist.

Hannah invited them to the backyard. She stopped, held open the back door, and waited for them to pass. She said, "I'll be right back. I have a pitcher of cool lemonade for us to drink. By the way, I hope everyone likes steak. I bought some nice T-bones for tomorrow."

Brandon saw Sarah and ran to her. He said, "Hi!"

Sarah tried to pick him up, but he turned and ran away. She thought, *"Whatever."*

Hannah called her friend Debbie and asked her to watch Brandon for the evening.

Debbie agreed. "I'd be glad to watch him. If it's easier for you, you could drop him off on your way to town."

Hannah thanked her, "You are such a big help to me. I can't thank you enough. We'll be there in a few minutes."

Hannah showed Sarah, Tina, and Joe a good time around town. They enjoyed delicious food and good drinks at a variety of Hannah's favorite places. They laughed and told funny stories about their childhood days.

Hours later, Hannah put her hands on her cheeks and complained. "My face is hurting from the constant smiling and laughing. Whew, this is so much fun."

They decided to finish the evening at the Motor Inn lounge.

Tina was visibly drunk. She grabbed Joe's arm and coaxed. "Come on, Honey, let's go to the room. I have a special delight for you."

Sarah laughed. "Lord, Tina! Are you in heat or something?"

Tina rubbed Joe's thigh and nibbled on his ear. "Grrrr, he's my man!"

Hannah said to Joe, "You better go, Mister, before she passes out."

Joe grinned, raised his eyebrows, and nodded in agreement.

Hannah smiled at Sarah. "I'd better be going, too. I still have to pick up Brandon. Will you be over early tomorrow morning?"

Tina had already corralled Joe towards the exit. She heard Hannah's comment. When she turned back to respond, she nearly fell. "Oops!" Joe grabbed her and kept her from falling.

Tina grinned at Hannah, and slurred, "We'll be there, that is, if I don't cause Joe to have a heart attack tonight!" She grabbed Joe's butt and giggled. She staggered slightly and waved. "Bye!"

Hannah raised her eyebrows, giggled at Tina, and waved. "Bye, Hun."

Joe grabbed Tina's butt and pushed her out the door.

Sarah snickered, "Those two are something else. They both act like teenagers. Tina should realize that she's not a kid anymore. She's more of an ump . . . teenager."

Hannah grinned and asked, "Ump-teenager, what do you mean by that?"

Sarah answered, "Duh; yes, an ump-teenager, umm, as in, ump-teen years old!"

Hannah chuckled, took a deep breath, and then let it out. "Love is grand, huh?"

Sarah said, "I suppose I should finish this drink and go to my room. I'll see you tomorrow."

Hannah hugged Sarah and gave her a kiss on the cheek. She stood up to leave. After a short pause, she looked at Sarah and asked, "Aren't you and I, ump-teenagers, too?"

Sarah gave a token toast with her drink, put her index finger to her lips and said, "Shhhh, don't tell anyone, but yes we are . . . but . . . we're not old yet . . . or, are we?"

Hannah smiled. "Whatever." She gave Sarah a quick hug, and left.

Sarah finished her drink and went to her room for the night.

Saturday morning, Tina and Joe were the worse for wear. Breakfast was of no interest to either of them. However, a strong cup of coffee and some Tylenol was a welcome sight for Tina's throbbing head and aching body. Sarah sipped her coffee and giggled at them. She watched poor Tina and Joe suffering from the effects of their night out. Joe said absolutely nothing; he could barely keep his head up.

Sarah asked, "Will you two be okay to follow me to Hannah's?"

Tina moaned, "Yes, but, please, don't drive too fast because I'm not sure if I remember where she lives." She moaned again. "Oh my God, I swear, I can feel my hair growing!"

Joe laid his head on his arms and rested on the table. He remained silent.

Sarah giggled again. "Drink up, we need to go. It's nearly noon now. I told Hannah we would be there at 9:30. She'll be throwing a fit."

Tina shook Joe. "Come on, Honey, you're driving."

Hannah waited for the cars to stop. She greeted Sarah with a hug, and led the way to the house. Tina and Joe followed, but stopped short of going inside. They sat on the porch steps.

Brandon raced through the house. He veered his way between Sarah and his mom. Without stopping, he jumped through the doorway and landed on the kitchen floor. Sarah noticed him, but said nothing.

Hannah said, "Mom called a few minutes ago. Apparently, her car won't start. She thinks the starter burned up or something. Her neighbor is trying to fix it. He thinks the problem is only a loose wire."

The phone rang, and Hannah answered it, "Hi, Mom." She asked, "Did he get it fixed?

No?

You'll need a new starter!

Well crap, nothing around here is open on Saturdays, especially past noon. Hold on, Sarah is here, I'll see what she wants to do."

Hannah held the phone against her breast and said, "Mom's car still won't start. She needs a new starter. Would you mind going with me to get her?"

Tina overheard the conversation and said, "You two go ahead. Joe and I will stay here. I'll watch Brandon until you get back. I can watch TV. Poor Joe needs a nap anyway."

Hannah nodded at Sarah. "Let's go get Mom."

Sarah agreed. "Okay, I can drive my car, but you will have to tell me where to turn."

Hannah put the phone to her ear. "Mom, Sarah, and I will come get you. If I take Rangeline Road, it will be an hour or so before I get there."

Marsha cautioned, "Be careful when you get near the reservoir. They've been redoing the pavement on Rangeline road. There's a stretch of about 6 miles that is only gravel."

Hannah said, "We'll leave in a few minutes and head your way."

Jokingly, Hannah teased Tina. "There are cans of coke in the fridge, and a fifth of rum in the cabinet." She chuckled. "Umm, just in case you get the urge for a good stiff drink!"

Tina moaned, "Oh my God . . . please . . . don't say anything about drinking for the rest of the day." She put her hand on her forehead. "My head is killing me." She waved her hand at Hannah. "Please, just go."

Hannah laughed, and then joked, "You poor babies!"

Hannah called for Brandon to come to her. She picked him up and said, "Mommy and your Aunt Sarah are going to go get your Grandma Marsha. We'll be back, soon.

You behave for Tina.

I love you." She kissed Brandon and hugged him. "You can play out back and Tina will be here if you need anything."

Sarah knelt and pinched Brandon's cheek. "You're such a cutie!"

Hannah kissed Brandon and said, "I love you."

Brandon kissed his mom and ran to the back yard.

Hannah looked at Sarah. "I'll get my purse, and we can go."

Sarah stood up to wait.

She watched Joe lie down on the couch and put his forearm over his eyes.

Hannah returned. "Okay, I'm ready."

Sarah giggled and said, "Tina, you partying sex fiend, it'll take Poor Joe all day to recover from last night."

Tina patted Joe's belly. "But he did so well; Grrrr."

Tina leaned over and kissed Joe. "He's my man."

Joe never budged.

Hannah snickered, "Please, spare me the details.

We'll be back in a couple of hours."

Hannah and Sarah left.

Sarah drove. She asked, "We're taking Rangeline Road?"

Hannah pointed. "Turn here. This way will be a little quicker to get on the highway. From there, it's only 3 miles to Rangeline."

Sarah asked, "Do you need anything from the store for tonight?"

Hannah said, "We might stop when we get back. I think I need some milk and probably some sour cream for the baked potatoes."

Hannah pointed again, and Sarah turned on to Rangeline Road.

Sarah rolled the windows down. "I love the smell of fresh country air. If it's too much air on you, let me know, and I'll roll the windows back up."

Hannah said, "It doesn't bother me." She set her purse in the back seat and said, "Beech Grove is 40 miles from here. If we went through Indy, it would be 63 miles, and traffic would be horrible."

Sarah drove slowly on the unfamiliar road. She complained, "This road is so narrow and curvy. Will it be like this all the way to Beech Grove?"

Hannah said, "Yep, but, we're in no hurry, right? Besides, it beats sitting in backed up traffic."

Sarah nodded in agreement.

Hannah took off her shoes and leaned her seat back a little.

Sarah read a sign, "Construction zone, 16 miles ahead, drive with caution."

Hannah remembered and said, "Mom says the road turns to gravel for about six miles when we get close to the reservoir."

Sarah looked at the sky through the windshield. "Is it going to storm? I thought I heard thunder."

Hannah said, "Maybe so. The weatherman on the news this morning was calling for storms to form today, and that some of them could be severe."

Sarah saw another construction sign. "No pavement, no shoulder, next 6 miles, drive with caution."

When Sarah drove on to the gravel roadway, a cloud of dust billowed up around the car. She slowed to nearly a stop. "What the hell?"

Hannah said, "It's only dust from the new limestone gravel they put on the road."

Sarah rolled up the windows and drove on.

Both girls screamed when a bolt of lightning flashed from the sky. The thunder rumbled through the car.

Sarah put her hand on her chest and exclaimed, "Wow that was close!" She leaned forward and looked at the sky through the windshield.

Hannah screamed, "LOOK OUT!"

Sarah jerked her head to look. A car was coming straight at her. She cranked the steering wheel hard to the right, trying to avoid a head-on collision. The oncoming car swerved in front of her. The front corners of the cars crashed together. The momentum forced the sides of both cars to slam against each other. Sarah's shoulder and head hit the door and side glass. Her car was out of control. The passenger door flew open. She screamed when Hannah fell from the moving car.

She watched in horror as Hannah tumbled across the gravel.

She saw the other car slide into the ditch and slam against a tree.

Her car spun down a steep embankment and came to a stop. She screamed, "Oh my God, oh my God," and even louder, "OH MY GOD!"

She panicked, and tried desperately to open the driver side door. It wouldn't budge.

She struggled across the front seat to the passenger side. She managed to crawl out. She tried to stand, but winced in pain. She fell to her knees. She grabbed her shoulder, and then her head. She could feel her heartbeat as the blood surged through the veins in her head.

Thunder rolled again, and rain began to fall.

Sarah grabbed the open passenger door, and labored to her feet. She called out, "Hannah! Oh my God! Hannah!"

Sarah looked to her left. The driver of the other car was a man. She watched him take two faltering steps and then fall to the ground.

Sarah crawled up the embankment. Her heart was racing.

She found Hannah.

Hannah was dead!

She began to cry.

She rose to her feet. She sobbed as she limped to where the other car had stopped.

The steady rain mingled with her tears and a trickle of blood, which ran down her face.

She realized, and said aloud, "I'm at the place of my Out of Body Experience." She wiped the rain from her eyes. Blood smeared across her face. "Oh my God, it can't be!" She squinted and tried to focus. She brushed the rain from her eyes again. She could see her reflection in the rear window of the man's car.

She stood over the man and began to whimper. Her body trembled.

She looked at her face again, and realized, "I'm alive!" She touched her face, and then the glass, which showed her reflection. Blood from her fingers trickled down the wet glass. She looked up when she heard a hissing sound. She smelled the odor of a hot engine. She glanced to her right, and saw the bullet-riddled sign. She studied it for a moment and then said aloud, "Range . . . line . . . Road!"

She looked to her left. Hannah's body lay motionless on the gravel. Blood dripped from Hannah's nose and ear. She saw the bloodstained shirt. A small puddle of blood had gathered beneath Hannah's head. The rain had washed blood down Hannah's face.

Sarah felt numb. Her legs were weak, and she could barely stand.

Lightning lit up the distant sky. Thunder rumbled through the cool damp air and shook the ground beneath her feet.

She looked to the sky and screamed at the top of her lungs. Her shriek echoed through the stillness. Her legs buckled, and she crumbled to her knees.

She stared at Hannah's lifeless body. She shivered in the cool damp air. Her skin felt wet and clammy. She whimpered in anguish, "Oh my God!

Oh my God!

No!

Please, no!"

Lightning flashed again, but no thunder sounded. She looked up and saw her car. Curiously, the black car now looked gray. She strained to her feet, and stumbled across the gravel. She stood and stared at the car for a moment. She swiped her hand across the fender. The gray limestone dust smeared away to reveal the black paint beneath. She exclaimed, "It wasn't gray!"

She winced in pain, turned, and limped back to Hannah. She began to cry again. A tear fell from her eye and dripped into a puddle of rain that had gathered near Hannah. She watched the ripples as they flowed across the surface of the water.

She remembered the man, and looked toward him. She squeezed her hurting shoulder and stammered, "This can't be happening." Her feet shuffled in the gravel as she walked to where the man had fallen. She stared at him. His face was in a pool of blood. He was not breathing.

Sarah wondered, "Who could this be?" She knelt, and rolled the man on to his back.

In awe, she cried out,

"DR. SHEFFIELD!"

The End

From:
brasshingepublishing.com
"Putting Words in Your Mind!"

Find it wherever fine books are sold.

From:
brasshingepublishing.com
"Putting Words in Your Mind!"

Find it wherever fine books are sold.

Discover other Stephen J. Flitcraft Books,
by visiting:

Brasshingepublishing.com